The Cl...
the Antiqu...

Nancy's friend Vera led the ... down a long hallway and through a bright, airy kitchen that looked as if it had recently been painted. "Julie," she called, "why don't you take a break and come meet—"

Vera's voice broke off as she reached the doorway on the far side of the kitchen. "Oh, no!" she gasped.

Nancy peered over Vera's shoulder. The big room looked as though a hurricane had ripped through it. Old furniture, tools, dolls, books, and clothing were strewn across the floor. A wooden captain's trunk was on its side, with a jumble of antiques spilling out of it.

Then Nancy saw something that made her breath catch in her throat. To the side of the overturned trunk was a young woman with short blond hair and very pale skin.

She lay motionless on the floor, her eyes closed.

Nancy Drew
Mystery Stories

Available from MINSTREL Books

NANCY DREW MYSTERY STORIES®

105

NANCY DREW®

THE CLUE IN THE ANTIQUE TRUNK

CAROLYN KEENE

A MINSTREL® BOOK

PUBLISHED BY POCKET BOOKS

New York   London   Toronto   Sydney   Tokyo   Singapore

This book is a work of fiction. Names, characters, places and incidents are either the product of the author's imagination or are used fictitiously. Any resemblance to actual events or locales or persons, living or dead, is entirely coincidental.

A MINSTREL PAPERBACK *ORIGINAL*

A Minstrel Book published by
POCKET BOOKS, a division of Simon & Schuster Inc.
1230 Avenue of the Americas, New York, NY 10020

Copyright © 1992 by Simon & Schuster Inc.
Produced by Mega-Books of New York, Inc.

ISBN: 0-671-73051-7

First Minstrel Books printing February 1992

10 9 8 7 6

NANCY DREW, NANCY DREW MYSTERY STORIES, A MINSTREL BOOK and colophon are registered trademarks of Simon & Schuster Inc.

Cover art by Aleta Jenks

Printed in the U.S.A.

Contents

1

Crime in the Country

"Wow! I had no idea the Berkshires were so beautiful," said Bess Marvin, pausing in the doorway of the bus. She brushed her blond hair out of her eyes and gazed at the snow-covered foothills that rose up before her in gentle waves.

"The evergreen trees smell great," Nancy Drew added, inhaling deeply. "Especially after two hours of breathing bus exhaust fumes and seat vinyl the whole way from Boston." She smoothed her shoulder-length reddish blond hair and stretched her long, slender figure.

Bess's cousin, George Fayne, gave Bess a nudge from behind. "Hey, would you mind getting out of the doorway? I'd like to get a look at this great view, too, if it's okay with you."

1

"Oh, sorry." With an embarrassed giggle, Bess lugged her big suitcase down from the bus and joined Nancy on the pavement. George quickly followed. A moment later, the bus door closed and the bus took off down the road, belching diesel fumes from its exhaust pipe.

"So this is White Falls, huh?" George set down her nylon bag and looked around. "No wonder Vera decided to move here."

The girls stood in a parking lot in front of a rambling wooden inn with a gabled roof. A row of old-fashioned storefront buildings stretched along the road beyond the inn. Several smaller roads wound up into the foothills, where Nancy saw a white church spire and scattered wood-frame houses. A river ran along the opposite side of the main road, its banks covered with snow.

"Vera's only lived here for two years," Nancy said. "She left River Heights when she inherited a house from her great-aunt here. Now she says she could never think of living anywhere else."

Nancy had remained in touch with her former neighbor, Vera Alexander, after Vera had moved to the small town in northwestern Massachusetts. When Vera had invited Nancy and her friends to White Falls for a traditional crafts fair, the girls had jumped at the chance.

"It looks like the perfect place for a crafts fair,"

Bess said. "I feel as if I've been plunked down in one of those paintings of old New England—you know, with sleigh rides and everyone cutting logs and feeding farm animals."

George groaned. "Nancy, can't you do something with her?"

"Actually, all that stuff is the reason Vera decided to move here," Nancy said. She couldn't help laughing at her friends. Although they were cousins and best friends, Bess and George were not at all alike. Blond, blue-eyed Bess's favorite activities were shopping and eating, but dark-haired George was more practical, with the tall, lithe build of a natural athlete.

Nancy flipped up the collar of her aqua ski parka. "But don't forget, the crafts fair isn't the only reason we're here. Vera was pretty vague about the details, but she did mention that someone might be trying to ruin the fair."

"Did she say why?" Bess asked.

Nancy shook her head. "That's one of the things I hope Vera can tell us. She should be here any minute."

Just then, a car horn sounded behind them. Nancy turned and saw a white minivan pulling to a halt in the parking lot. The driver's door flew open, and a tall, slender woman in her thirties hopped out, her long black hair spilling around the collar of her red ski parka.

"Nancy!" the woman called, running over and giving her a hug. "I'm so glad you could come."

"Me, too, Vera," Nancy said with a grin. "It's great to see you. You remember Bess and George."

Vera shook the girls' hands and said, "Sorry I'm late, but I had to drop off some speakers for tonight's barn dance."

Bess's blue eyes lit up. "A barn dance?" she asked. "You mean square dancing?"

"You bet," Vera told her. "I thought it would be a good way to kick off the crafts fair. There's a maple syrup boil tomorrow, the crafts workshops on Saturday, and then a big auction on Sunday."

"Sounds great," George said.

"It ought to be." Vera's smile faded as she added, "As long as nothing happens to ruin it, anyway."

Nancy gave Vera a sympathetic look. "What makes you think something will happen?" she asked.

With a sigh, Vera reached for Bess's suitcase. "Here, let's get your stuff into the van. I can explain while we drive to my house."

A few minutes later, Nancy was seated beside Vera in the van's front seat. Bess and George settled on the bench seat behind them.

"The whole reason I decided to organize this crafts fair was to raise money for a pet project of mine," Vera began as she pulled out onto the road

4

that ran along the river. "I want to open a museum, dedicated to the local people and their history."

"I remember you mentioned that in your letter," Nancy said. "You're going to renovate an old building for the museum, right?"

"It sounds like a terrific idea," Bess put in.

Vera smiled ruefully at Bess in the rearview mirror. "I'm not sure everyone agrees with you. About a week ago, I started receiving threatening phone calls telling me that if I don't back off the project, someone will make sure my museum never opens. The voice is always muffled, and I can't tell if it's a man or a woman."

"And you think whoever it is might ruin the fair so you won't have enough money to fix up the building," George guessed.

Vera nodded. Nancy could see that Vera was definitely upset about the threats.

"Do you have any idea who's making the calls?" Nancy asked.

Vera took a deep breath and let it out slowly. "There are some people who seem to be against the project—or maybe I should say one person in particular."

Leaning forward on the bench seat, Bess asked, "Who's that?"

"A real estate developer named Rosalind Chaplin. If you ask me, Roz is much more concerned with making a buck than with preserving White Falls's heritage. She's constantly tearing down beautiful old buildings and replacing them with modern monstrosities that have no character whatsoever.

"Needless to say," Vera continued, her dark eyes flashing with indignation, "Roz had different plans for my museum site. She wanted to bulldoze the old building and put up condos for the ski crowd. When they put it to a vote, the town decided on the museum, but Roz seems to hold it against me personally that her plan wasn't chosen."

"Hmm," Nancy said. "I'll definitely keep my eye on her. Is there anyone else you can think of who might have a grudge against you?"

Vera shrugged. "Not offhand. New Englanders are a tough bunch to figure out, though. They tend to keep their thoughts and feelings to themselves, especially around strangers."

"Oh, look!" Bess exclaimed, pointing. "There's one building that Roz Chaplin hasn't gotten her hands on yet."

Looking out the van window, Nancy saw a large stone building perched on the far bank of the river, just above a crashing waterfall. Covered with ivy and nestled into the snowy woods, the building looked to Nancy as if it had been there since the beginning of time.

"Well, at least *someone* around here has good

taste," Vera said, a wide smile spreading across her face. "You're looking at what will one day be the White Falls Historical Museum," she announced proudly.

"That's going to be your museum?" Nancy asked, impressed. "It looks as if it has a lot of history of its own."

"Oh, it does," Vera told her. "If those old walls could talk, I'm sure they'd have plenty of stories to tell. There was even a murder that took place there, you know."

"A murder?" George asked. She looked at the stone building with fresh interest.

"It was a long time ago," Vera added quickly, glimpsing in the rearview mirror the horrified look on Bess's face. "The building used to be an old knife factory called Caulder Cutlery. The owner, Zach Caulder, was stabbed to death right in his office, with one of his own knives. The police never did find out who did it."

"Stop! It's too gruesome!" Bess exclaimed, covering her ears.

"The factory's been quiet for over fifty years now," Vera assured her. "It went bankrupt soon after Zach died, and the town took it over. It's been empty ever since."

Vera turned onto a side road that curved up into the hills, away from the river. Drifts of snow lined the road. After rounding a few bends, she pulled the van into a plowed gravel driveway behind a small bright yellow car. "Here we are," she announced.

Beyond the snow-covered yard Nancy saw a three-story white house with a porch running along the front. Bushy shrubs and huge oak trees separated the house from its neighbors. Warm light glowed from inside the large shuttered windows.

"I think I could get used to staying here," George said. She, Nancy, and Bess grabbed their suitcases and followed Vera along the short path that had been shoveled and up the stone steps to the porch.

"It's huge," Bess added. "Doesn't it feel strange to be rattling around in such a big house all by yourself?" she asked Vera.

Vera shook her head. "Not really. I know it sounds strange, but all the crafts and antiques I've collected over the years make me feel as though I have plenty of company.

"Besides," she went on, "Julie Bergson, my assistant, is here most days. She's been helping me organize everything for the museum and the crafts fair. Sometimes I think I wouldn't be able to find my own head without her help." She nodded to the yellow car in the driveway. "Julie must still be working—that's her car."

As the girls stepped into the front hallway behind Vera, Nancy saw the living room through a doorway. It was very comfortable looking, filled with a

8

jumble of old-fashioned furniture, lamps, pillows, and tables.

"Julie?" Vera called. When there was no answer, she said to the girls, "I've converted a big workroom in the back into storage for the fair and museum. She must be back there."

Vera led the way down a long hallway and through a bright, airy kitchen that looked as if it had recently been painted. "Julie!" she called again. "Why don't you take a break and—"

Vera's voice broke off as she reached the doorway on the far side of the kitchen. "Oh, no," she said with a gasp.

Rushing across the kitchen, Nancy peered over Vera's shoulder. The big room off the kitchen looked as though a hurricane had ripped through it. Old furniture, tools, dolls, books, and clothing were strewn across the floor. A wooden captain's trunk lay on its side, with a jumble of antiques spilling out of it.

Then Nancy saw something else that made her breath catch in her throat. To the side of the overturned trunk was a young woman with short blond hair and very pale skin.

She lay motionless on the floor, her eyes closed.

2

Robbed!

"Julie!" Vera cried, running toward the unconscious woman.

Nancy was only half a step behind. Her heart
pounding, she bent over Julie and checked her
pulse.

"Nancy, is she . . . dead?" Bess asked from the
doorway, the final word coming out in a high
squeak.

"No," Nancy answered with a sigh of relief. "Her
pulse is strong, and she's breathing easily. Quick,
get a wet towel from the kitchen."

A moment later, Nancy was applying the cool,
moist towel to Julie's forehead. The woman looked
as if she was in her early twenties, with straight
blond hair cut chin-length. As Nancy held the towel

10

to her forehead, Julie groaned, moving her head slightly. Then her eyes fluttered open.

"What—?" Julie blinked a few times, her green eyes clouded with confusion. Then she snapped her head up sharply, looking fearfully from Vera to Nancy, Bess, and George. "Oh, no," she said in a horrified whisper.

Nancy put a calming hand to Julie's shoulder. Obviously the young woman was disoriented.

"Take it easy," Vera said gently, grasping Julie's hand. "It's me, Vera, and these are my friends, the ones I told you were coming."

Julie reached up unsteadily and, wincing, touched the back of her head. "But how did—?" She broke off as she saw the disorganized mess of the workroom. "Oh, no," she said again.

Vera shook her head. "Don't worry about the mess," she said. "We'll clean it up later."

"No! I mean, it's not about the mess," Julie said. Her green eyes flitted nervously around the workroom as she pushed herself to a sitting position. "It's much worse. Vera, that black lacquered chest, the one that was donated last week—it was right by the desk."

Vera's gaze flew to the desk, and the color drained from her face. "It's gone," she said.

"I stored some antique patchwork quilts in that trunk," Vera told Nancy and her friends in a distraught voice. "They were exquisite one-of-a-kind pieces, worth over a thousand dollars each. They were going to be one of the big draws at Sunday's auction. There's no way I can replace them."

"It looks as though whoever made those threats was serious about wanting you to back off the museum project," George said. She pointed to a rooster-shaped cast-iron weather vane that rested on the floor near Julie. "He or she must have hit Julie over the head with that."

Vera nodded, blinking back tears. "This is just what I was afraid of. But at least you're okay, and that's what really counts," she said, squeezing Julie's hand. "I could never forgive myself if . . ." Her voice trailed off. For an uneasy moment, no one said anything.

"Maybe we should get Julie some water or something," Bess suggested, breaking the silence.

"That's a wonderful idea," Vera agreed. She gave Bess a grateful look. "In fact, I think we could all use some hot cocoa. I'll make some right away. And, Julie, I want you settled on the living room couch."

"Bess and I can take care of that," George offered. With George on one side and Bess on the other, they helped Julie to her feet.

Nancy stayed behind as her friends and Julie left the workroom. "I'll catch up with you in a minute," she told Vera. "I just want to take a quick look around here first."

Nancy carefully scanned the workroom, and the first thing she noticed was a dolly standing next to the door. Its wheels were still wet, as if it had been rolled through the snow outside. There were wet tracks on the floor, too. Nancy followed them into the kitchen and out a back door.

Outside, she picked up the dolly's tracks in the snow and followed them around the house to where they stopped at the gravel driveway. The thief must have loaded the trunk into a car or truck and simply driven away, Nancy realized. Since the driveway had been plowed, there were no tracks for Nancy to check. And with the thick shrubs on either side of the house, it was unlikely that Vera's neighbors would have seen anything.

When Nancy went back inside, Vera was measuring cocoa into a pot of steaming milk on the stove. Nancy returned to the workroom and walked slowly around it, being careful to sidestep the dusty toys, old blankets, and ruffly Victorian dresses. The place was a mess, but she didn't see anything unusual.

With a sigh, Nancy crossed her arms and leaned against the kitchen doorway. If the thief had wanted to steal the quilts, why did he or she make such a mess of everything else, too? Or had the person done this as a warning to Vera to give up her museum project?

"Any luck?" Vera asked. She was holding a tray with five mugs of hot cocoa on it.

"Not really," Nancy told her. She pointed to the dolly next to the doorway. "At least the thief had the courtesy to return your dolly after using it to cart the trunk out of here," she said. "I didn't find any clues as to who did it, though."

"I feel awful that this happened to Julie in my house," Vera said, shaking her head. "Things have been hard enough in her life already."

Nancy caught the worried expression in Vera's dark eyes. "What happened to her?" she asked Vera.

"Julie told me she used to be . . . well, a bit troubled back in high school," Vera replied. "I think she got caught up in a bad crowd. That's all over with now, though," she added quickly.

Nancy didn't want to pry, so she gestured toward the mugs of cocoa on Vera's tray. "I guess we'd better join the others before those get cold."

As Vera nodded and disappeared through the kitchen, Nancy took one last look around the workroom. Then something on the doorframe caught her attention. There, about six inches up from the floor, was a deep nick in the fresh yellow paint.

Bending down, Nancy carefully examined the dent. A few slivers of wood with a shiny black covering were stuck to the doorframe. Could they be from the stolen trunk?

Nancy went back to the front of the house and found the others in the living room. Julie was

14

stretched out on the couch, a faded quilt spread over her legs, and a glass of water on the coffee table beside her. Vera perched on an arm of the couch, holding a fresh towel to Julie's forehead.

"Did you find anything?" George asked. She and Bess were on a love seat by the fireplace, sipping their hot cocoa.

Nancy told them about the nick in the doorway. "It looks as if our thief knocked the chest into the doorway between the workroom and kitchen on his way out." She glanced at Vera. "Unless you remember that dent being in the doorframe already."

Vera shook her head as she held out a full mug of cocoa for Nancy. "I just painted the doorway this morning."

"It doesn't tell us who stole the trunk, though," Nancy said with a sigh. She took the cocoa and sat down in an armchair. "That's where you come in, Julie. Did you see or hear anything unusual before you were knocked out?"

Julie gave Nancy an apologetic look. "I don't really remember much. One minute I was logging in some things on our computer inventory. The next thing I knew, I was waking up with you guys standing over me, and the workroom looked like a national disaster area."

"You don't even remember hearing the door opening?" George asked.

"Sorry," Julie said, shaking her head. "My back

15

was to the door. With the hum of the computer, I guess I didn't hear the person come in."

Nancy took a sip of her hot cocoa. "It certainly looks as if the attack was aimed at your crafts fair," she told Vera. "But we can't rule out other possibilities." Turning to Julie, she asked, "Do you know of anyone who might want to hurt you?"

"I don't th-think so," Julie answered slowly. "No one that I know of, anyway."

"Goodness me, it's already four-thirty!" Vera exclaimed, looking at her watch. "The barn dance starts at seven, and I've got a million things to do." Jumping up from the couch, she waved her hand toward the back of the house. "All that mess will have to wait until morning. Julie, you stay right where you are. And as for you girls," Vera added with a nod to Nancy, Bess, and George, "let's get you settled in your room upstairs."

"I can't dance another step," George said that evening as she and Nancy finished a square dance. George's face was flushed from dancing.

Nancy nodded. "We haven't stopped dancing since we got here. Let's take a break."

The two girls thanked their dance partners and stepped to the side of the huge barn. The wide wooden floor planks had been swept clean from the big sliding doors on one side to the hayloft on the other. A low platform was set up along one wall for

16

the musicians. Two fiddle players started in on their next song, and a robust, gray-haired man called out the first steps.

Nancy noticed a boy with curly dark hair being ushered toward the musicians by an older woman. He looked about eleven years old. From the scowl on his face, Nancy guessed that he wasn't happy about being at the dance. The woman, who looked stern and tight-faced, pushed him up onto the platform.

There was quick applause from the dancers as the boy reluctantly joined the fiddle players, pulled out a harmonica, and began to play along. Though he played quite well, it was obvious from the way he glared at everyone that he was performing against his will.

Nancy tapped her foot in time to the music and watched the dozens of couples bowing to each other and beginning to dance. She was glad to see Vera among the dancers, though Nancy noticed her friend's gaze sliding worriedly around the barn. Julie had recovered enough to attend. She was sitting on the edge of the musicians' platform.

"What happened to Bess?" Nancy asked George, her eyes skimming over the crowd. "Oh, there she is, next to—"

"The refreshment stand," George finished with a grin. "Where else would Bess be?"

Nancy grabbed George's arm and began pulling

17

her toward the tables that had been set up in the alcove beneath the hayloft. "I could use a drink, too. Come on."

"Hi, you guys," Bess greeted them, waving a cup in her right hand. "You should try some spiced cider—not to mention these desserts." She held out a small plate in her other hand. "I couldn't make up my mind, so I took one of everything."

"Mmmm, is that a brownie?" George asked, plucking a chocolate square from the plate.

"Save some for me," Nancy told them. "I'll get us some drinks, George." Leaving her friends, Nancy headed toward a table where there was a punch bowl filled with steaming apple cider.

She was just leaning over to get some cups when a high-pitched yapping at her feet caused her to jump back with a start. Looking down, she saw a miniature white poodle in a frilly plaid outfit, its tail wagging as it jumped around Nancy's feet.

"Fifi, come here at once!" bellowed a forceful female voice. A moment later, a thin red-haired woman in a red tweed suit and high heels scooped up the dog, holding it protectively in the crook of her arm.

The woman gave Nancy a critical look. "You're here for this silly crafts fair, I suppose," she said.

Nancy blinked, slightly taken aback. "Yes, I am," she answered. "My name is Nancy Drew. I'm a friend of Vera Alexander."

18

The woman's hazel eyes narrowed. "Oh, really," she said, her voice dripping with disdain.

Nancy just stared at the woman. Clearly she didn't think much of Vera or the festival. Nancy couldn't help wondering why the woman had bothered to come to the barn dance at all—unless it was to cause trouble.

"And are you . . . ?" Nancy asked.

"Rosalind Chaplin," the woman replied with an annoyed sigh, as if Nancy should already know her.

"Take it from me," Roz went on. "Vera Alexander is just a nosy newcomer who's trying to make a big splash with all her plans for White Falls. The last thing this town needs is a stupid museum." Roz leaned forward and pressed her face close to Nancy's. "And you can bet I'll do everything I can to make sure it doesn't open."

With that, Roz readjusted the poodle on her arm and stalked away.

Nancy frowned as Roz's red tweed suit disappeared into the crowd. The woman had said almost exactly the same thing that the anonymous caller had told Vera.

Quickly filling two mugs with cider, Nancy rejoined Bess and George. "Hey, you guys," she said, handing George her cider, "I just met our top suspect."

"Roz Chaplin?" George scanned the crowded barn. "Where?"

19

"She's wearing a red suit," Nancy answered. The developer seemed to have been swallowed up by the crowd, but Nancy did see Vera. The musicians had taken a break, and Vera was talking to one of them near the refreshment area.

A few straws of hay wafted down from the hayloft above her, but Vera merely batted them away and continued her conversation.

Looking up, Nancy saw that the bales of hay in the loft above Vera were trembling. Suddenly one of them rocked wildly, tipping toward the edge of the platform and sending a shower of straw to the floor below.

The next thing Nancy knew, the huge bale was tumbling over the edge of the loft—heading straight toward Vera!

3

A Harmonica in a Haystack

"Vera! Look out!" Nancy shouted. She hurtled across the refreshment area, grabbed Vera by the waist, and dove with her to the side. Both of them hit the floor with a thud.

A split second later, the floor shook as the bale of hay crashed down exactly where Vera had been standing.

Nancy untangled herself from Vera and brushed some loose strands of prickly hay from her face. "Vera, are you okay?" she asked breathlessly.

The force of the fall had thrown Vera flat on her back, and her hair was a confused swirl covering her face. As Vera pushed the long strands back, Nancy could see a glimmer of fear in her dark eyes.

"I th-think so," Vera stammered. "How on earth did that happen?"

Nancy looked up at the loft again, but the hay now appeared quite still. "Someone must have pushed one of the bales," she said angrily.

Nancy jumped to her feet and began pushing through the crowd that had gathered around them. Then she sprinted up the wooden stairway that led to the loft, pausing at the top to let her eyes adjust to the dimness.

Bales of hay were stacked three and four deep along the back and side walls of the loft, and loose straw littered the open center. Some of the bales were close to the edge of the loft, but Nancy was sure they couldn't just fall over by themselves. On the other hand, she didn't see anyone, or any spot where the culprit could hide.

As Nancy began sifting through the loose straw for clues, a sudden blast of cold air hit her back, making her shiver. She turned and peered into the shadows of the back wall. She could just make out the gleaming metal of a door latch and a sliver of star-studded sky.

Hurrying over to the spot, Nancy found a wooden door between some bales of hay. It was open a crack. She carefully peeked out through the opening. The top of a ladder was propped up to the loft door from outside, its rungs glistening in the moonlight.

"So that's how the person got away," she murmured aloud. Still, no one was on the ladder, or anywhere Nancy could see on the snowy ground below.

"Did you find anything?"

Nancy turned to see George at the top of the stairs. "The escape route, but not the attacker," Nancy told her, pulling the door shut again.

As she walked toward Nancy, George scanned the dim hayloft. "Hey, what's this?" she asked as her foot hit a shiny metal object in the loose straw. She bent down and picked it up. "A harmonica! That's funny. Here, take a look."

"A harmonica? I wonder if . . ." Taking the small instrument from George, Nancy went over to the top of the stairway. Down below, the lively strains of music had started up again. "Remember that boy who was playing the harmonica," Nancy said excitedly, looking down at the musicians' platform. "He seemed really angry before, and now he's gone."

George looked at Nancy skeptically. "Do you really think a kid pushed that bale of hay?" she asked. "Why would he want to hurt Vera?"

"I don't know," Nancy admitted. Her eyes were still focused on the dance floor below, where another square dance was in progress. Vera, Bess, and Julie were sitting it out, talking quietly together.

Nancy's gaze lit on a red tweed suit near the

23

barn's sliding door. "That's weird," Nancy said softly. "Hey, George. Look at Roz Chaplin."

"What about her?" George asked, spotting Roz.

"Doesn't she seem kind of nervous to you?" Nancy said. "She keeps looking over at Vera. And look at her dog."

Roz had Fifi in her arms and was brushing frantically at the poodle's plaid costume. Then, with a last look over her shoulder at Vera, Roz disappeared through the barn door.

George drew in her breath sharply. "Her dog's covered with straw! Maybe Roz was the one who knocked over that bale. If you ask me, that'd make more sense than a kid being responsible. Maybe this harmonica isn't even his."

"Maybe," Nancy replied, turning the small instrument over in her hand. "I know one thing for sure, though. I'm going to have to find out more about both of them."

"So you really think Roz might be the one who's after Vera?" Julie asked the next morning. She had arrived at Vera's house just as Nancy, Bess, and George were finishing up the breakfast dishes. Now they were all helping Vera sift through the mess in the workroom.

"I don't have any proof yet, but I wouldn't be surprised if Roz is up to something," Nancy answered. She brushed back her reddish blond hair with a dusty hand. "I also want to question that harmonica player I told you about, Vera."

Nancy held up an extravagant hat made of maroon velvet, ribbons, and feathers. "Is this for the museum or the crafts auction?" she asked.

"Oh, that's gorgeous," Bess crowed. "They sure made things fancier in the old days."

"Smaller, too," George said dryly. She was peering doubtfully at a tiny satin lady's shoe in her hand. "I might be able to squeeze my big toe in here, but that's about all." With a shrug, she asked, "Where should I put this, Vera?"

Vera chuckled as she pointed to the far end of the workroom, where a row of labeled cardboard cartons was arranged along the wall. "All of the clothes are for the museum," she said. "You'll find the boxes back there. The crafts, like quilts and boxes and anything made of wood or iron, are stored on this side of the room, near the door."

Turning back to Nancy, Vera said, "As for the harmonica player, his name is Mike Shayne. I hired him a few months ago to run errands. He did a great job until about two weeks ago, and then . . ." Vera frowned, letting her voice trail off.

"He was stealing money from Vera, so she had to fire him," Julie finished. The young woman sat down at the computer and began typing inventory items from a list on the desk.

Nancy raised her eyebrows. "Really?"

25

Vera nodded. "Every time I gave Mike ten or twenty dollars for an errand, he returned with only a fraction of the change I knew I should have gotten. When I confronted him about it, he admitted to stealing the money, but he wouldn't explain why." Vera sighed, plucking at the cotton of a quilt she was folding. "I would have lent him the money if he'd asked, but under the circumstances I felt I had to tell his aunt and uncle—"

"Not his parents?" Nancy interrupted.

Vera shook her head. "His mother and father died in a plane crash when Mike was a few years old. He's lived with his aunt and uncle ever since."

"I see," Nancy said thoughtfully.

"If you want to talk to him," Vera went on, "you might try Shayne's General Store. Mike's aunt and uncle own the place. School's on vacation this week, and Mike helps out there in his free time."

"What about Roz's office?" Bess asked. "Where's that?"

"You'll need to drive there, I'm afraid," Vera told the girls. "Why don't you take my van? The maple boil isn't until two, so I won't need it until after lunch."

Nancy smiled at her old neighbor. "Thanks, Vera."

Vera placed some folded clothes inside a wooden captain's chest and closed the top. "You're sure you wouldn't rather see some of the local sights?" she asked. "We don't have much, but you might want to visit Esther Grey's house."

"The poet?" Bess asked eagerly. "We studied her work in tenth grade. I forgot she lived in White Falls."

Vera nodded. "Her house is quite close to here."

Nancy brushed the dust from her jeans and stood up. "I think for now we'd better concentrate on finding the person who stole that trunk yesterday," she said.

"Not to mention whoever's been threatening you, Vera," George added. "And the person who pushed that bale of hay." She turned to her cousin. "Sorry, Bess. Maybe we'll go to Esther Grey's house later."

The girls were about to leave when Bess paused next to the computer table. "Oh, look," she said, picking up an old leather volume with the initials ZC stamped on its cover in gold. "What a beautiful old book."

"I'll take that," Julie said, taking the book from Bess. Then, seeing Bess's look of surprise, she explained, "Sorry, I guess I get overprotective of all the stuff here. It's funny. I never even look at any of these things—they're just entries in the computer inventory to me. But until something's logged on the computer, I feel very responsible for it."

"Logging it in will only take a second," Vera said. She crossed over to the computer desk and took the book from Julie. "Besides, I've already noted it on the list I gave you. I'm sure it won't hurt for Bess to take a look at this."

From Julie's expression, Nancy guessed that she didn't agree with Vera. But she didn't say anything more as Vera handed the book to Bess.

"You might find it interesting," Vera said. "It's Zach Caulder's diary."

Bess's eyes widened. "You mean the guy who was murdered?"

Vera nodded. "It was donated by the town just recently. I haven't even had a chance to read it yet, but I bet it's fascinating."

As Bess began flipping through the diary, George tugged on her arm. "Later, Bess. We're on a case, remember?"

"Okay, okay," Bess replied. She tucked Zach Caulder's diary in her bag, then followed her friends out the workroom door. "Bye, Vera. Bye, Julie," she called over her shoulder. "And thanks for lending me the diary."

Following Vera's directions, the girls drove down the curved, snow-lined road to Main Street, which ran along the river. Shayne's General Store was a wide, low storefront between the post office and a farm equipment store. The girls stomped the snow from their boots, then went inside.

A bell jingled as they entered. A stern-faced woman at the checkout counter glanced up and said hello. Nancy saw that it was the same woman who had forced Mike to play the harmonica at the barn dance. She smiled and said hello to the woman as they passed.

Wide wooden shelves ran up and down the store in rows. They held everything from groceries to gardening tools to rain ponchos. An old-fashioned soda counter stretched along the wall to the right. The counter had a faded, red fake-marble top and aluminum stools with peeling red vinyl seats.

"There he is," George said in a low voice, gesturing to the boy behind the soda counter. Nancy immediately recognized the curly-haired boy. He was bent over a comic book, his elbows propped on the counter.

"And look what's behind him," Bess added in an excited whisper.

Nancy glanced at the shelf behind the counter, where a harmonica lay. "I wonder if that's the same one he played last night," she whispered back. "Let's find out."

As the girls sat down, the curly-haired boy looked up from his comic book. Up close, Nancy saw that he had big brown eyes and a round face. "Oh, hi," he greeted them, standing up straight. "Can I get you something?"

Nancy and Bess ordered vanilla milk shakes, and George chose chocolate. As the blenders whirred,

Nancy turned to Mike. "You're a pretty good harmonica player," she told him. "We heard you playing last night at the barn dance."

A slight frown came over Mike's round face. "My aunt made me go," he grumbled. "But I knew that dance was going to be awful, just like the rest of the dumb crafts fair." He shoved his hands into his jeans pockets. "I even lost my harmonica there. I had to buy a new one today."

Nancy reached into her parka pocket and pulled out the harmonica she'd found in the hayloft. "Is this it?" she asked.

"Hey!" Mike shot Nancy a leery glance as he grabbed it from her. "Where'd you get that?"

"In the hayloft at the barn dance," Nancy said.

Mike shook his head in disgust. "I can't believe someone stole it from me and left it up there," he said.

The boy sounded sincere, but Nancy couldn't be sure he wasn't just saying that to throw them off. She decided to try a different approach. "Mike, someone pushed a bale of hay at Vera Alexander last night. She could have been badly hurt if it had hit her."

For a moment Mike just glared at Nancy. Then he said angrily, "It's too bad it missed her. Vera's ruining everything!"

Without another word, Mike took his comic book

to the very end of the counter. He continued reading it there, studiously ignoring them.

Shooting a backward glance at her friends, Nancy picked up her milk shake and walked to Mike's end of the counter. "You don't seem to like Vera very much," she said gently. "Why not?"

Mike's brown eyes flashed with anger. "It's none of your business," he said. "And you should tell Vera to mind *her* business, too. She'd better stay away from Caulder Cutlery—if she knows what's good for her!"

4

A New Twist

Nancy exchanged looks with Bess and George. Why would Mike care about Vera's plans for Caulder Cutlery?

"What do you mean?" Nancy asked Mike. "Are you talking about Vera's project to turn the factory into a museum?"

The boy gave Nancy another icy stare. Then he stormed to the back of the store, disappearing through a doorway that looked as if it led to a storeroom.

"Wow," Bess said, stirring her milk shake with her straw. "Talk about touchy!"

Still gazing in the direction of the storeroom, Nancy murmured, "I wonder if—"

"I must apologize for my nephew's behavior," a tight, worried voice interrupted.

The girls turned to find the woman from the checkout counter standing next to them. She was twisting the hem of her grocer's apron in her hands. "Mike has been such a trial to us lately. I'm afraid I don't know quite what to do with him."

"No harm done," George said pleasantly. She finished the last of her milk shake and put the glass on the counter.

"You're Mike's aunt?" Nancy asked. The answer seemed obvious, but Nancy wanted to get the woman talking about him.

The woman nodded curtly. "I'm Grace Shayne. My husband and Mike's father were brothers. I just don't understand it," she said, the worry spilling from her voice. "Up until recently, Mike has never been a problem. But during the last week or so . . ." She broke off with a sigh.

That was about the time Vera had started receiving the threatening phone calls, Nancy realized. "What has Mike been doing?" she asked.

"Oh, skipping school, avoiding his chores here at the store, disappearing at odd hours," Mrs. Shayne replied. "And the boy refuses to give any explanations." She shook her head critically. "He's looking for trouble, if you ask me, the same way his grandfather did."

As the woman spoke, she seemed to become more agitated. "Charlie Shayne was a bad apple if there ever was one," Mrs. Shayne went on. "Maybe it was never proven, but everyone knows he's the one who killed Zach Caulder."

Nancy looked at her friends in surprise. She knew it would be impolite to pry, but she couldn't resist asking Mrs. Shayne, "You mean the man who was murdered in the old knife factory?"

Mrs. Shayne covered her mouth with one hand. "Oh, my," she said nervously. "I shouldn't be talking this way. Charlie is my husband's father, after all. It's just that I get so mad thinking about the terrible thing he did."

"Maybe he didn't do it," George suggested. "I mean, how could people be so sure Charlie killed Zach Caulder if the police couldn't prove it?"

Mike's aunt pressed her lips together in a tight line. "I wish I could believe that," she said grimly. "But people saw Charlie leave the factory the night of the murder. And when he left town right after that, it was the same as admitting he was guilty." She gave a bitter snort before adding, "Of course, he left the rest of the family here to live with the shame of what he did. I just hope he doesn't ever come back."

Nancy drummed her fingers on the faded red countertop. She couldn't help feeling sorry for Mike's aunt. But right now she had a case to solve.

34

She was trying to turn the conversation back to Mike when the jingling of bells at the store's entrance announced another customer.

"Oh, dear," Grace Shayne said worriedly. "Here I've been rambling instead of keeping an eye on things. Excuse me, girls." With that, she rushed back over to the checkout counter.

"What a story," Bess said once she, Nancy, and George had paid for their milk shakes and were back out on Main Street.

"Mmm," Nancy said. She sighed as she zipped up her parka. "It's too bad we couldn't get more of the story on Mike, though."

"I know what you mean," George said. "So why do you think he wants Vera to stay away from Caulder Cutlery?"

Nancy took the keys to Vera's van from her jacket pocket. "Maybe he thinks the cutlery will remind everyone that his grandfather might be a murderer."

"Maybe," George said thoughtfully. "Anyway, I'm beginning to think you're right about him pushing that hay down on Vera last night. Did you see how mad he got when you mentioned her name?"

George looked amused when she saw the faraway look in her cousin's eyes. "Earth to Bess. Are you there?"

"Oh, I guess I was daydreaming," Bess admitted,

shaking herself. "I keep thinking about Zach Caulder. I mean, the whole story's so amazing, and I even have his diary right here." She tapped her bag, then looked sheepishly at her friends. "I can't help wondering what the man was like. Would you guys, um, mind if I didn't go with you to Roz Chaplin's office?"

Nancy laughed. "Let me guess. You can't wait a second longer to start reading that journal. Sure, Bess, we'll meet you back at Vera's for lunch."

"There it is," George said, pointing as Nancy pulled into the parking lot of a short strip of new-looking stores and offices on the outskirts of White Falls. A sign that read Chaplin Real Estate Development hung outside an office at the end of the strip. Nancy parked Vera's minivan in front of it.

Getting out of the van, Nancy and George paused to look at the photographs of houses and commercial buildings that were taped to the office's front window.

"No wonder Roz hates Vera's museum project," George commented. She pointed to a modern metal-and-glass condominium building. "Roz's idea for White Falls is totally different from Vera's, that's for sure."

Nancy nodded. "The question is, how far would Roz go to keep Vera's plan from succeeding?"

The girls entered the office just as Roz strode

purposefully out of a back office, followed by an eager young man with slicked-back blond hair. The man was wearing a gray suit and taking notes furiously on a large pad.

"And then I need you to check up on the crew at the Olmstead Street renovation," Roz said over her shoulder. "Arnie told me the refrigeration is being installed today."

The real estate developer frowned as she saw Nancy and George standing inside the door. "Oh, it's you," Roz said. She seemed anything but pleased to see them. "Nancy Drew, right?"

Nancy nodded. "And this is my friend, George Fayne. We'd like to talk to you for a moment, if you don't mind."

Roz waved her hand impatiently. "Can't you see I've got a million things to take care of here? I couldn't possibly—"

"We'll be very quick," Nancy promised.

Roz opened her mouth as if to object, but then she seemed to think better of it. "This way," she said, showing Nancy and George into her inner office. She sat behind a desk with a smoked glass top and motioned for the girls to sit in the two leather and chrome chairs.

Glancing around the small room, Nancy didn't see a trunk, but she didn't really expect Roz to leave a stolen trunk where anyone could see it.

Nancy wasn't sure what to say, so she decided to

be direct. "I don't know if you're aware that Vera Alexander has been receiving threats to drop her plans to renovate the Caulder Cutlery factory into a museum," Nancy began.

A satisfied smile rose to Roz's lips. "It's nice to know I'm not the only one who has the sense to oppose her plans," she said.

The developer didn't seem surprised by the news, but it was hard to tell for sure. Nancy leaned forward in her chair. "A wooden trunk of quilts for Sunday's auction has been stolen," she added.

"Not to mention that Vera was almost knocked over by that bale of hay last night at the dance," George put in.

Nancy nodded, then turned back to Roz. "You wouldn't happen to know anything about that, would you?"

Roz looked quickly from Nancy to George. "It was probably an accident," she said smoothly, but Nancy noticed her fingers fidgeting nervously with some papers on her desk.

"I don't have to resort to those kinds of tactics," Roz went on. "My business is more of a success than any project of Vera's will ever be. By modernizing old farm buildings and houses, I'm helping to bring new industry to White Falls."

"You mean, by totally destroying beautiful old buildings," Nancy said before she could stop herself.

38

Roz's smile faded to a dark frown. "You've been spending too much time talking to Vera. She's getting everyone all excited over that worthless museum project of hers."

"But don't you think White Falls's history is worth preserving?" George asked. Nancy could tell her friend was fighting to keep her temper.

"My family has lived in this area since the seventeen hundreds," Roz said haughtily. "Some of my relatives are world-famous. I'm as proud of my heritage as anyone." She paused. "I just don't see any use in harping on the ancient past. What we really need in White Falls are modern buildings and businesses for the future."

Just then the young man stuck his head in the doorway. "Ms. Chaplin, the furniture for the ski condos is here," he said.

"It's about time," Roz said, getting quickly to her feet. "I'd better see to the unloading myself." Nancy thought the woman seemed relieved for an excuse to end their conversation.

"Do you mind if we tag along?" Nancy asked.

Roz shot her an annoyed look. "I suppose it won't do any harm," she said.

Nancy and George followed the developer down a hallway and through a door that led to a garage. A big truck had pulled up to the garage's outside door, and two men were unloading black couches and chairs wrapped in protective plastic.

"No, not there!" Roz called. Her heels clicked on the cement floor as she hurried over to one of the moving men and tapped him on the shoulder. "Over there," she ordered, pointing to a clear section along the garage wall. "Can't you people ever get anything right?"

"What a dragon!" George whispered to Nancy. "The way she's hounding those guys, I wouldn't blame them if they decided to drop that stuff right on her."

Stifling a laugh, Nancy glanced around the garage. Sleek, modern furniture, unopened packing crates, and rolls of carpeting and fabric were scattered in no special order. Seeing that Roz was still badgering the furniture movers, Nancy began strolling around the garage, keeping an eye out for a black lacquered trunk.

She had just taken a few steps when a growling noise behind her made Nancy pause. Instinctively she tensed. But when she turned around, she saw that it was only Roz's little dog, Fifi. The white poodle was half-hidden behind a wooden crate. Its teeth were clamped around one end of what looked like a blanket that the dog was pulling from side to side, as if she were doing battle with it.

"Oh, isn't she a cute little thing," George said softly.

"Fifi, the mighty warrior," Nancy joked. A moment later, she drew in her breath sharply. Fifi had dragged the blanket farther out, revealing a multi-colored star pattern. "George! Look, it's a quilt!"

George stared at Nancy as if she had lost her mind. "Yeah. So?"

"So, what's an old patchwork quilt doing with all this modern stuff?" Nancy asked excitedly. "And look where Fifi's pulling the quilt *from!*"

George's brown eyes widened with understanding as she saw what Nancy was pointing to. The trunk was mostly hidden behind the wooden crates, but one black lacquered corner was visible. George whistled softly. "Vera said the stolen trunk was a black lacquered one with quilts inside," she said.

Nancy nodded triumphantly. "I think we've found our thief!"

5

Found—and Lost

"Let's take a look," Nancy told George in a low voice. "If we find yellow paint on that trunk, we'll know for sure that it's the one that was stolen from Vera."

"You mean the paint would show from where the trunk nicked the new paint in the doorway?" George asked.

Nancy nodded and took a step toward the trunk. In the next instant, however, she was jostled to the side as Roz swept past her.

"Fifi! Let go of that," Roz scolded, scooping up the little dog and prying the quilt from Fifi's mouth. Then she grimaced, holding a corner of cloth between her thumb and forefinger as if it were some

42

sort of slimy rag. "What is *this* old thing doing here?" she asked disdainfully.

Roz's gaze fell on the black trunk, and Nancy saw her face freeze for a second. Then, just as quickly, Roz turned toward Nancy and George and began hustling them away from the trunk.

"It's a lovely quilt, Roz," Nancy commented, trying to resist the woman's insistent pushing. "I'd love to take a closer look at it." She peered back over her shoulder at the trunk, trying to see if there were any signs of yellow paint.

But Roz ushered her and George firmly back into the office. "I'm sorry, girls, but I have to get back to work now," she said. Nancy thought she detected a slight note of nervousness in the developer's voice. "Perhaps another time."

Before Nancy and George knew what was happening, Roz had led them to the front door of the office and ushered them outside. "Good day, ladies," she said, closing the door behind them. Nancy watched through the window as Roz stormed through the doorway to her private office and disappeared inside.

"We were so close," George said, stamping her foot in frustration. "I bet anything that was the trunk from Vera's."

Nancy hurried to the side of the real estate office in time to see Roz's assistant close the garage door.

43

Apparently the delivery men had just finished unloading the furniture. They were climbing back into the front of their truck and starting the engine.

Nancy let out a discouraged sigh. She and George would have to wait for another time to get a closer look at the trunk.

"There's something I don't understand," Nancy said, going back to George. "Roz seemed as surprised as we were when she saw the trunk. I mean, if she knew about it, why would she let us go out to the garage in the first place?"

George shrugged. "Maybe she figured it was hidden well enough behind those crates," she suggested. "If Fifi hadn't drawn our attention to it, we probably wouldn't have seen the trunk. I bet Roz was just pretending to act surprised to throw us off."

"I guess you're right," Nancy said, pulling the keys to Vera's van from her purse. "Anyway, there's nothing more we can do here now. We might as well head back to Vera's."

"Bess, hurry up!" George called. "We don't want to be late for the maple boil."

"Especially since I promised Vera we'd be on the lookout for any trouble," Nancy added. "We won't be able to spot much of anything if we're not even there."

The two girls were waiting in the front hall of Vera's house, wearing jeans, scarves, gloves, and heavy sweaters. Right after lunch, Vera and Julie had driven over to the farm where the demonstration would take place. Vera had left Nancy directions to the maple farm, saying that it would be a pleasant walk.

Nancy could hear doors and drawers banging upstairs in their room. Soon Bess raced down the stairs, pulling on her parka, hat, and gloves as she went.

"Sorry," she said breathlessly. "I got so caught up with my reading that I forgot about making maple syrup this afternoon."

George shot her cousin a look of total disbelief. "You *forgot* about tasting one of the yummiest things in the world?"

"I didn't think any book could be that good," Nancy teased as the girls left the house, locking the door behind them.

"Me neither, but I guess I was wrong," Bess said. "You guys should get a look at Zach Caulder's diary. You wouldn't believe how juicy it's getting. I mean, at first it was kind of boring—you know, mostly just a log of the factory's expenses, how much cutlery was produced every day, stuff like that. One thing comes through loud and clear, though. Old Zach was very cheap. He wrote him-

45

self tons of reminders to watch over his foreman and the workers to make sure they weren't stealing from him."

"Maybe he had a good reason to be careful," Nancy said. "After all, he *was* murdered."

"Ooh, don't remind me," Bess said with a shiver. "Anyway," she went on excitedly, "now Zach is starting to write more personal stuff. He's being wooed by a mystery woman. Someone left flowers in his car at the factory last night, along with an anonymous love note."

George rolled her eyes. "Bess, I hate to disappoint you, but Zach Caulder's been dead for over fifty years. You're talking about this guy as if he's still alive."

Bess smiled sheepishly at her friends. "I guess reading his diary makes me feel as if he is." Then she shook her head. "If Zach *were* alive, though, I don't think I'd want to know him. He sounds like a real miser."

The girls crossed over Main Street, and their boots crunched on the snow as they started on the pedestrian walkway of the bridge over the Deerfield River. About halfway across, Bess paused to lean against the safety railing. Her eyes were on the stone factory perched on the opposite bank, above the falls.

"I'm so glad Vera's making Caulder Cutlery into a museum," she said.

46

"It *is* a beautiful building," Nancy agreed. The ivy over the old factory was so thick, it almost completely covered the structure, but Nancy could make out indentations where sunlight glinted on glass windows. There were two rows of four windows each. For a moment she enjoyed the view, letting her gaze wander over the woods that hugged the cliff on either side of the factory. Then her eyes rested on the bright white of a snowy clearing, and the colorful jackets and coats of the people gathered there. "Come on, you guys," Nancy said.

They hurried the rest of the way across the bridge and entered a snowy gravel drive marked Owens Maple Farm. Circling around a wooden farmhouse, the girls found themselves in the clearing Nancy had seen from the bridge. The day was fairly warm, but several inches of snow still covered the ground and the branches of the surrounding trees.

The participants were spread out in different groups. Some were collecting sap into wooden barrels on sleighs. Others were pouring the sap into a huge cast-iron pot that hung over a low fire. A handful of men and women wearing green Owens Maple aprons over their sweaters seemed to be directing the various demonstrations.

At one side of the clearing, a raised trough had been filled with snow. Vera was helping a group of children pour the hot syrup into shapes that hardened into maple sugar on the snow. She had a scrapbook of old photos and engravings of New England "sugaring off" gatherings, which she was showing to the children.

"There you are," Vera said, smiling as the girls walked over to her. "Julie just went back to the house to do some more computer work. She had strict orders to send you three up here right away. I didn't want you missing one of the best parts of the whole crafts fair."

"Mmmm," Bess said, sniffing the sweet, maple-scented air. "I hope someone's making pancakes to put all this syrup on."

Vera laughed and pointed back toward the farmhouse. "As a matter of fact, Trisha Owens is whipping up a huge batch right now."

As Bess and George joined a group collecting sap from the wooden taps in the sugar maple trees, Nancy scanned the area. Sunlight glinted off the snowy clearing, and Nancy shaded her eyes with her gloved hands to see better. So far, so good, she thought as she gazed at the different groups of people. The maple boil seemed to be going smoothly.

Suddenly Nancy tensed. Out of the corner of her eye she spotted a flash of blue and red at the edge of the clearing. Looking more closely, she recognized Mike Shayne's curly, dark hair above his blue jacket and red high-top sneakers. He was circling the edge of the clearing, looking furtively at Vera every couple of seconds. Even from fifty feet away, Nancy could see the angry glint in his eyes.

What's he up to? she wondered, slipping quietly across the clearing toward him.

A moment later Mike's eyes widened as they focused on Nancy. The boy broke into a run and tore off into the woods, disappearing behind a thick clump of evergreens.

In a flash, Nancy was after him. Snowy branches slapped at her face as she followed Mike's footsteps through the dense, dim woods. She couldn't see him, but the sounds of branches snapping up ahead told her she wasn't far behind.

After about twenty yards, Nancy saw that the boy's footprints had merged with other prints in what looked like a small path. Either Mike or someone else had been on it recently. Soon the path opened out into a clearing. Nancy paused to get her bearings, her chest heaving from running.

In the center of the clearing, an ivy-covered stone building rose two stories high. The building was perched right at the edge of the high riverbank. It was the Caulder Cutlery factory, Nancy realized.

Mike's footprints didn't lead to the factory's wooden double doors, as she would have expected. Instead, they pointed in the opposite direction, around the side of the building. As Nancy began to follow the prints, she heard a rustling noise, then the squeaking of hinges.

Picking up her pace, Nancy circled to the side of the factory—and stopped short. There, about half-way along the factory wall, the footprints abruptly ended.

Puzzled, Nancy gazed up at the factory's outside wall. The smooth surface of ivy-covered stone didn't seem to be broken by any window or door. It was as if Mike had disappeared into thin air.

Think, Nancy, she told herself, frowning. There had to be a way in. Stepping closer to the wall, she brushed her gloved hands through the thick tendrils of ivy, working her way over the entire area next to the last set of footprints. About four feet above the ground, her hand caught on something metallic. Pushing the ivy aside, Nancy found a small window set into the stone, its glass thick with dust and grime.

Nancy's heartbeat quickened as she pushed in the window. It gave way with a creak of its rusty hinges. A moment later, she climbed up and through the window, dropping to a wooden floor. The sound echoed in the cavernous space.

Peering around, Nancy saw that she was standing in a large room that must have been the factory's main work area. It was now empty of any equipment or workbenches, though some rusty metal bins and loose debris had been swept into one corner.

Nancy didn't hear any movement. Some light filtered through the windows, though, and she was able to spot wet footprints leading across the floor. A rickety-looking wooden stairway at the far end of the room led up to a wide balcony that jutted out over the main floor. A second stairway led downward from the main level, into a basement.

Had Mike gone up or down? The wet footprints dried out before the stairs, so it was impossible to tell. Nancy glanced up toward the three doorways off the upper balcony, but she decided it would be better not to risk the rickety stairs unless she had to.

Crossing over to the basement stairwell, Nancy gingerly tested the top step with her foot. It creaked but seemed solid enough. Feeling along the wall with her hands, Nancy made her way carefully down the black, shadowy stairwell. The stairs turned, finally opening out into what had once been a storage room.

The three windows in the lower level provided some light. Nancy quickly saw that Mike wasn't there. Like the main level above, the room had been emptied of whatever it had once held. Only the bare shelves that lined the four walls remained.

A loud grating noise from somewhere above her

startled Nancy, and she hurried back toward the staircase. She had only gone a few steps up the narrow staircase when a deafening metallic clatter rang out above her. As she stuck her head around the bend in the stairwell, Nancy's breath caught in her throat.

One of the rusty metal bins she'd seen on the main level was hurtling down the staircase toward her!

Nancy jumped backward, but the step gave way beneath her boot, throwing her off balance. As she toppled back toward the floor, the large metal bin clanged around the bend in the stairs. In seconds it would come crashing down on her head!

6

History Repeats Itself

Nancy hit the floor with a thud. Gritting her teeth, she tucked her slender frame into a ball and rolled out of the barrel's path. A moment later, the metal bin clattered harmlessly past.

Breathing deeply, Nancy got to her feet and made her way slowly up the staircase, rubbing her sore hip. She reached the main floor just as a pair of red high-tops disappeared through the ivy-covered window she'd used to enter the factory.

"Mike! Stop!" she shouted. But her only answer was the creak of the window's hinges as it swung shut after the boy.

With a disappointed sigh, Nancy sat down on the top step to examine her hip. It was tender to the

53

touch, but she didn't think any real harm had been done.

Then she looked curiously around the factory. Mike had already made one threat about the factory, back at the general store. Could he have been the person making the threatening phone calls to Vera, too? But even if he was, Nancy didn't see what he could accomplish by sneaking into the factory. Vera hadn't started the renovation yet, so there wasn't even anything to ruin.

"Nancy! Where are you?" called a familiar voice from outside the factory's front doors.

"George, is that you?" Nancy shouted. She rose to her feet and hurried to the double doors, still rubbing her hip. "I'm in here!"

She could hear mumbling on the other side of the doors, and the rattling of doorknobs. Then Bess's voice said, "It's locked. Nancy, how did you get in?"

"Around the side," she called through the doors. She was about to explain where to find the window in the ivy when she heard a third person join George and Bess. Nancy couldn't distinguish the new voice, but she heard the scrape of a metal key in the front door lock. A moment later the double doors opened, and Bess and George rushed anxiously toward Nancy. Julie Bergson was with them.

Nancy hugged her friends. "Boy, am I glad to see you!" she exclaimed.

"Nancy, are you okay?" Bess asked.

"We got worried when you disappeared from the maple boil," George said. "Some woman said she saw you take off after Mike Shayne. We scouted around and found the tracks in the snow."

"I'm fine," Nancy assured them. "No thanks to Mike," she added grimly, as she rubbed her hip. "He just tried to steamroll me with one of those bins over there."

Pointing to the remaining metal bins in the corner of the main floor, Nancy explained what had happened. "I'm pretty sure Mike's been here before," she finished. "There were several sets of footprints leading to the window."

"I've never seen him here," Julie said. "In fact, except for the inspectors, I've never seen anyone here but Vera and me." Frowning, she added, "This place isn't safe for a kid by himself. I'm going to nail that window shut. And I guess Vera or I will have to talk to Mike to make sure he understands he can't come back here."

"Good idea," George agreed. "Hey, Nan, do you think Mike's being here has anything to do with what he said this morning? You know, about Vera staying away from the factory?"

"There must be *some* connection," Nancy told her, "but I don't have any idea what it is." Turning to Julie, she asked, "Can you think of any reason

55

why Mike wouldn't want Vera to renovate Caulder Cutlery?"

Julie shook her head. "I know he's mad that Vera told his aunt and uncle about his stealing money from her. But I never heard him say anything against the museum." She shrugged, then added, "He's just a kid. Maybe he comes here to play."

"I'm pretty sure he was running away from me," Nancy said. "That's not how a kid acts when he's just playing."

"All's well that ends well," Bess said brightly. "What are you doing here, anyway, Julie? I thought Vera said you had more computer work to do."

Julie nodded. "I do, but it'll have to wait. Vera needs some measurements for a meeting with the architect," she said, taking a tape measure from her jacket pocket.

"Why don't we help you?" Nancy offered. "As long as we're here, we might as well make ourselves useful."

"No, no," Julie said. "Thanks, but you three should go back and enjoy the rest of the maple boil."

"Actually, I'm not that hungry anymore," Bess said. She sighed, "I can't believe we're standing in the actual factory where Zach Caulder was killed."

"Oh, brother," George muttered to Nancy. "Here she goes again."

Julie pointed to one of the doorways on the balcony level. "As a matter of fact, Bess, Zach's office was right up there."

"Oh, let's go see it," Bess said, hurrying toward the stairway.

"Stop!" Julie ordered. Bess and Nancy looked at the blond woman in surprise.

"Vera's afraid of anyone using those steps until they've been reinforced," Julie explained.

Bess glanced dubiously at the rickety wooden staircase. "They do look a little shaky."

"Besides, I think we should get Nancy back to Vera's house," George put in. "She should definitely have that hip checked out."

"Why don't you take my car?" Julie offered. "That way you can stop at Dr. Jennings's office. It's just off Main Street."

Nancy started to protest that a doctor wasn't necessary, but Bess and George were already thanking Julie and pulling Nancy out the door.

"And don't worry about Vera," Julie called after them. "I'll stop by the Owens farm on my way back and tell her where you are."

"*Now* are you satisfied that I'm okay?" Nancy asked her best friends as she climbed gingerly back into the front seat of Julie's yellow car. Nancy had had to wait over an hour to see the doctor. There

57

was a flu going around, and it seemed that half the town had caught it.

"Dr. Jennings said no unnecessary moving around until tomorrow," Bess reminded Nancy. "So you're definitely not going to the White Falls Inn tonight to hear Vera's talk about the museum."

Nancy had been looking forward to hearing more about Vera's plans for Caulder Cutlery, but she knew her friends weren't about to let her out of the house. "Just because I can't go doesn't mean you can't," she told Bess and George.

"And leave you all alone? No way," Bess said loyally.

"The maple boil is probably over by now," George said, glancing at her watch as she pulled onto Main Street from the parking lot. "I guess we should head back to Vera's."

As they drove, Nancy tried to make sense of all that had happened so far. Roz Chaplin seemed the likeliest suspect for the stolen trunk. But then, why had Mike thrown that barrel at her? And who was making the threatening phone calls to Vera? Was it possible that Roz and Mike were somehow working together?

Nancy's thoughts were interrupted as George suddenly braked, causing Nancy to lurch forward. She glimpsed the tail end of a car that had cut across their lane onto a side street.

"Are you guys okay?" George asked. She shook her head in disgust. "The guy could have tried signaling."

"Wasn't that a police car?" Nancy asked, leaning forward to get a better look at the black and white car. "It's turning down Vera's street. I hope everything is okay."

"His lights weren't flashing," George pointed out. "It's probably just a patrol car making its regular rounds." But Nancy noticed that George pressed the gas pedal down a little more.

"Uh-oh," Nancy said under her breath as they rounded the final curve before Vera's house.

Sure enough, the police car had parked in front of Vera's house. A female officer was standing on the porch with Vera, who looked very distraught. As soon as she caught sight of Julie's car, Vera ran over.

"Nancy, are you all right? Julie told me what happened to you at the factory."

"I'm fine," Nancy assured her, getting out of the car. "But what happened here?"

Vera's dark eyes filled with tears. "It's awful. I can't believe it's happened again. When I came back from the sugaring off, I went to the workroom to return this," she explained, waving the scrapbook in the air. "I keep it on a shelf above a wooden captain's chest."

Nancy nodded. She remembered having seen the chest the day before.

"The trunk had several pieces of irreplaceable vintage clothing in it," Vera went on.

Bess gasped. " 'Had'? Do you mean . . . ?"

Tears spilled down Vera's cheeks. "It's gone!" she cried. "Another trunk has been stolen!"

7

Fascinating Reading

"Another trunk is missing?" Nancy repeated in disbelief. She exchanged worried looks with Bess and George.

"Roz must have stolen it when Julie went over to Caulder Cutlery," Vera said, angry spots of color rising to her cheeks. "After you and George saw that black lacquered trunk at her office this morning, I just know Roz took this one, too. Well, she's not going to get away with this. I'm going over there right now."

"That might not be a good idea," Nancy said quickly. "We don't know for sure yet that Roz is responsible. And if you accuse her without proof, she might raise a fuss that would give bad publicity to the crafts fair and your museum."

"Oh," Vera said, frowning. "I hadn't thought of that."

Just then, the police officer came up to them. A pleasant-faced woman with wavy auburn hair and a smattering of freckles across her nose, she introduced herself as Officer Margaret Conroy.

"I don't see any signs of forced entry," Officer Conroy said, making a few notes on a pad she carried.

"I'm sure we locked up when we left for the maple boil," George told her.

The policewoman shrugged. "Unfortunately, many thieves are quite good at picking locks. Now, what did I hear about this Roz someone? Is she a suspect?"

Vera looked uneasily at Nancy. "Well, sort of," she said. "Yesterday another trunk was stolen from me. I'm afraid I've been so caught up with the crafts fair that I didn't even report it yet."

"George and I think we might have seen the trunk when we were at Roz Chaplin's office today," Nancy added. "But we don't know for sure, and we don't want to risk making a false accusation that could result in bad publicity for the crafts fair."

Officer Conroy shook her head, giving Vera a dubious look. "If that's the way you want it, we won't investigate at this point. But I'll put a call in to the station and make sure an officer is posted at all crafts fair events from now on."

"Thank you," Vera said gratefully.

"And we'll be sure to call if we see anything suspicious," Nancy told the policewoman.

After Officer Conroy had taken Vera's statement, Vera led the others back into the house.

"Let's hope there won't be any more trouble today," she said. "I knew the crafts fair would be exciting, but things are getting out of hand."

"Vera, are you sure you don't want Bess or me to go with you?" George asked Vera that evening as she was getting ready to leave for her talk on the museum project.

"Thanks, but I'll be fine on my own," Vera told them. Nancy was stretched on the sofa, and Bess and George were lounging nearby on a rag rug. A bowl of popcorn and three glasses of soda were on the coffee table.

Vera smoothed her maroon sweater dress and picked up a leather pouch that held the proposed plans for the White Falls Historical Museum. "I see Julie came and picked up her car," she said, peering out the front window.

Bess nodded. "She arrived while you were changing. She said she'd meet you at the White Falls Inn for the presentation."

Vera smiled. "Julie's been such a good friend to me, and a real help. She's the one who keeps things organized around here. Like today, for instance. I never would have thought of taking those measurements for the architect's meeting. The meeting's not for another week and a half. Julie's a great one for getting things done ahead of schedule."

"You mean, you didn't send her there?" Nancy asked.

Vera shook her head. "No, but it's just like Julie to take care of things like that so I won't have to worry about them. Well, I'd better be off. See you later." With a wave, Vera disappeared out the front door.

Nancy took a handful of popcorn and settled back against the comfortable sofa cushions. Bess was already engrossed in her reading.

"I guess you and I are going to have to keep each other company," Nancy told George. "Bess seems to be spending the evening with Zach Caulder."

Bess was so absorbed in the diary that she didn't even look up.

"Hey, what's this?" Bess murmured a moment later. Nancy looked as Bess lifted a crinkled, yellowed paper from the diary and carefully unfolded it.

"Wow, the mystery woman wrote Zach a poem!" Bess exclaimed. "Listen to this." She bent excitedly over the paper, reading it aloud:

"Oh, to find a soul so sweet,
Two hearts moved by a single beat.

64

Oh, brightest star!
I need no light but thee.
Thy love, and mine,
Shall bind us for eternity."

Refolding the paper, Bess put it back in the worn
leather diary. "Isn't that romantic?" she said with a
sigh. "Boy, I'd give anything to have a guy write me
something like that."

"You know, hearing that poem gives me an idea
about who the mystery woman was," Nancy said,
biting her lower lip thoughtfully. "Do you think it
could have been Esther Grey?"

Bess's blue eyes lit up. "That's right! Vera told us
Esther Grey lived in White Falls. I remember from
high school English that she never did marry. I bet
it *was* her."

George took a sip of her soda, crunching down on
the ice cubes. "Well, whoever it was, it sounds as
if she wanted to marry Zach Caulder," she commented.

"Zach wrote something about that," Bess said,
nodding. "But he didn't seem very happy about it."
She flipped back a few pages in the diary, running
her finger down the entries. "Here it is. 'My secret
admirer must think I'm a fool,'" Bess read. "'She
writes of love and marriage. Hah! She's no better
than the others. What she truly loves is not me, but
the money I have worked so hard for.'"

"That poem didn't sound like it was written by a fortune hunter," George put in. "Zach Caulder must have been a total jerk."

Nancy nodded. "He sure seemed suspicious of everyone—especially when it came to money."

"Well, I think that stinks," Bess said emphatically. "He doesn't deserve to have someone writing him poetry."

As Bess and George talked about Zach Caulder and his mystery admirer, Nancy's mind turned back to the case. She hated having to keep still. Someone could be trying to harm Vera or the crafts fair at that very moment, and Nancy still didn't know who the person was. The auction was just two days away. If Nancy couldn't get the stolen trunks back before then, it might seriously hurt the auction's success.

Nancy sighed. One thing was for sure. Tomorrow she'd have to find a way to get another look at the trunk in Roz's office garage.

A sudden gasp from Bess jolted Nancy out of her thoughts.

"Let me guess," George said dryly. "Zach had his own mother arrested because she borrowed a nickel and didn't give it back."

Bess looked up at her friends without laughing. "Now Zach thinks that the mystery woman is trying to murder him," she said in a horrified whisper. "I can't believe she'd do it, but—"

"*Someone* killed him," Nancy reminded Bess. "What does he say?"

Turning back to the diary, Bess said, "Okay, here goes. 'My secret admirer tells me that if she can't marry me, then no one else shall have me, either. I fear for my life.'"

Bess gave Nancy and George a worried look before continuing. "'Her scheme will not succeed. I won't allow her or anyone else to cheat me out of my riches. My money is hidden where no banks or lawyers or other moneygrubbers will ever find it. If need be, the secret of my money chest will die with me.'"

Bess shook her head. "That's the last entry. You guys, maybe this is the last thing Zach ever wrote in his life. I bet he was murdered by the mystery woman right after this."

"Wait a minute, Bess," George put in. "I really don't think the mystery woman was the kind of person who would kill someone for his money. That was just in Zach's head."

"Maybe she killed him out of jealousy," Bess said stubbornly. "She did tell Zach that if she couldn't have him, she'd make sure no one else could."

George shrugged. "What about Charlie Shayne? According to Grace Shayne, people saw him leave the knife factory right after the murder."

As the cousins argued, a warning bell went off in

Nancy's mind. She had the feeling there was an important connection that she was missing. But what was it?

"That's it!" she exclaimed suddenly, sitting bolt upright on the couch.

"*What's* it?" George asked, frowning.

Turning to Bess, Nancy said excitedly, "The diary says something about a secret money chest, right?"

Bess nodded, a puzzled expression in her blue eyes.

"Well, that must mean Zach hid all his money in some kind of chest or trunk," Nancy went on. "What if whoever killed him didn't even know about his money, or wasn't able to find it?"

"I guess it would just stay in his secret chest, then," George said, shrugging.

A spark of interest lit Bess's eyes. "Hey, maybe it's still around somewhere, with all the money in it."

Nancy nodded. "That's just what I was thinking. Zach's murder may be related to our case!"

"What?" Bess and George both exclaimed.

"Bess, maybe you're not the only one who read Zach's diary," Nancy went on. "Anyone who did would find out that he hid his money in a trunk."

George snapped her fingers. "And two of them have suddenly been stolen from Vera!"

"Right," Nancy said. "Maybe whoever's stealing these trunks isn't trying to sabotage Vera's museum project at all. Maybe he or she is trying to find the secret money Zach wrote about in his diary!"

8

Hidden Clues

"Wow," Bess said. "So now we have to figure out who could have read the diary, right?"

"Vera and Julie have both seen it," George said. "But I think we can eliminate them. I mean, they wouldn't have to steal the trunks. They could just examine them right here."

"We can't eliminate anyone without proof," Nancy cautioned. "But Roz Chaplin and Mike Shayne do seem like better candidates.

"I think Vera said that the Town of White Falls donated the diary," Nancy said. "Let's go back to the workroom and see if we can find out anything else about it."

Nancy led the way back through the kitchen and flicked on the workroom lights.

"There must be a half dozen trunks in here," George said, surveying the room. "I mean, how would the thief figure out which one the money is in? He can't just go around stealing every old trunk in White Falls."

"We'll have to check the computer inventory to see if we can trace the missing trunks, too," Nancy told her. "Maybe there's some connection between them and the diary."

Going over to the computer station, Nancy sat down and flicked the On switch. As the computer whirred and beeped into action, she glanced at the row of binders lined up along the edge of the desk. She grabbed one marked Inventory and opened it to the first page.

"Here's a note from Julie explaining how to use the computer system," Nancy said, glancing at a note card taped to the binder's inside cover.

George came up behind Nancy and read over her shoulder. "You can access the inventory by date, by different categories of items, or by the name of the person who donated the things."

"Let's see if there's a category for diaries." Nancy typed a few commands into the keyboard. A moment later, the screen was filled with entries of diaries, memoirs, and letters that had been donated for the historical museum. They were listed in alphabetical order.

"Here it is," Nancy announced, scrolling down to

the Cs. " 'Caulder, Zachary.' It says here that his diary was donated by the Town of White Falls on March first—that's last week."

"That doesn't tell us much," Bess said from the other side of the room, where she was examining a battered-looking chest. She came over to join Nancy and George. "Anyone could have read the diary if it was in the town hall or some public place like that."

"Let's see what else we can find out," Nancy suggested. She exited from the category menu, then typed in the commands to pull up the inventory listing according to donations. "Here we go," she said as the blinking cursor stopped next to the "Town of White Falls" entry.

The three girls scanned the list of donations that had been made by the town the week before: old tools, a grinding stone, casting equipment for cutlery. "This stuff was originally in Zach Caulder's factory," Nancy murmured. "The town must have received it when the factory went bankrupt after Zach died."

"You know, it seems kind of funny that Caulder Cutlery went bankrupt, since Zach had so much money," Bess said.

Nancy nodded. "But the money was hidden in his secret money chest, remember? Zach said he didn't want anyone to find it. If no one discovered the money after he died, that would explain why the factory closed."

"Hey!" George exclaimed, pointing at the glowing screen. "Look what else the town donated—a wooden captain's chest and a black lacquered trunk."

Nancy's heart skipped a beat as she read the entry. "That means there's a connection between the diary and the missing trunks," she said. "They all belonged to Zach Caulder."

Bess nodded. "So now we're looking for someone who knew those two trunks belonged to Zach Caulder *and* who could have read the diary." She looked expectantly at her two friends. "Any brilliant ideas?"

"It looks like we're back to Vera and Julie," Nancy said, frowning. "They would know where everything came from. But as you said, George, they wouldn't have had to take the trunks away."

"Besides," George added, "Julie said she only looks at this stuff long enough to log it on the computer. I doubt she would have read the diary."

"What about Mike Shayne?" Bess suggested. "Vera said he used to help her out. If he was working here when the stuff from Caulder Cutlery was donated, he might have gotten a look at the diary."

Nancy nodded. "And he would know which trunks to search, too. We'll have to ask Vera when she fired him. If it was after the end of February, that would make him more of a suspect than ever."

George snapped her fingers. "And that would explain what he was doing at the factory, too. Mike must have been looking to see if another trunk had been left there somehow."

Putting her elbows on the desk, Nancy cupped her chin in her hands. "I think we should find out all we can about Zach's murder," she said, thinking out loud. "Tomorrow we can pay a visit to the local paper, or the library, to look for newspaper issues dating back to the murder."

When her friends didn't answer, Nancy looked up and saw that George was frowning. "What's the matter, George?"

"I was just trying to figure out how Roz Chaplin might fit into all of this," she said slowly. "I mean, we *did* see that trunk in her office, but how could she have known any of this stuff about the diary and the money and the trunks?"

"Good question," Nancy agreed. "And if someone's after the money, why would they try to hit Vera with a bale of hay, or make those threatening phone calls?"

She sighed and stared back at the computer screen, as if it could give her the answers she needed. "I wish there was a way to find out if anyone else went through the things from the factory before they were donated. Maybe that's how Roz knows about Zach's money."

Nancy blinked as she realized what she was

staring at. "Wait a minute," she said. "Here it gives the name of the person who made the arrangements to donate the things from the factory. Rosemary Norris, a member of the town council—"

"And the curator of the Esther Grey House," George finished, reading from the screen.

"You're kidding!" Bess exclaimed. "Do you think that means there's definitely a link between Esther Grey and Zach Caulder?" she asked.

"Not necessarily," Nancy cautioned. "Rosemary Norris was acting on behalf of the town when she donated the things, not on behalf of Esther Grey. There's still no proof that there was any kind of relationship between Zach and Esther Grey."

Nancy's next words were cut off by a huge yawn. "I guess we'd better get some sleep, guys," she said. "First thing in the morning, we're going to visit Esther Grey's house!"

Rosemary Norris was one of the tallest, most graceful women Nancy had ever met. She wore a pleated navy skirt and a white blouse, and her gray hair was swept back into a knot at the nape of her neck. As she led the tour through Esther Grey's home, it was obvious that she was very proud of the town's famous poet.

"And here we have the study where Esther Grey wrote most of her poetry," Mrs. Norris said, gesturing to a room on the second floor.

Nancy looked around as she, Bess, and George followed the half dozen other tourists into the room. Bookcases lined every inch of the four walls that wasn't taken up by the fireplace, the windows, or the door. The only pieces of furniture were the desk, a worn leather reading chair, and a small sofa.

"As I mentioned earlier, Miss Grey's great poetic talent wasn't discovered until after her death," Mrs. Norris said. "She was a very private person who lived alone here from the age of forty-two, when her mother died, until her own death at seventy-eight.

"Esther Grey also had one sister, but they did not see each other often," Mrs. Norris added. "Most of the poet's waking hours were spent right here in this room, writing."

The man standing in front of Nancy raised his hand. "For a woman who never married, Esther Grey certainly wrote a lot of love poems," he observed.

Mrs. Norris nodded slowly, and a sad smile spread across her face. "Just because she never married doesn't mean she was never in love," she said. "Many people believe that Esther Grey was in love with a man who did not return her feelings."

Nancy felt an elbow jab her in the side and heard Bess draw in her breath sharply.

"If the story is true, it must have been quite tragic," Mrs. Norris went on. "But I suppose that her romantic feelings inspired Miss Grey to write as much poetry as she did." Mrs. Norris gestured toward a large, ornately covered wooden box that rested on the desk. Its lid was open, revealing hundreds of yellowed papers. "These are all love poems to an unnamed man."

"Does anyone know who that man was?" George spoke up from behind Nancy.

"Literary scholars have debated the question for decades," Mrs. Norris replied. "There have been rumors of all sorts, but no one knows for sure who the man was, or if he even existed. These poems might simply have been a way for Esther Grey to unburden her lonely heart."

Mrs. Norris took a framed poem from the wall and handed it to a woman at the front of the group. "The poet's living relatives have never published any of the love letters and poems, so we have framed one to show visitors."

When the framed poem reached Nancy, she read it eagerly, with Bess and George looking over her shoulder.

"Hey, this poem mentions 'love's brightest star' and 'kindred spirits' who 'follow the same drummer's beat,'" Nancy whispered. She looked expectantly at her two friends. "Sound familiar?"

George nodded. "It's a lot like that poem Bess found in Zach Caulder's diary," she said.

"I knew it," Bess whispered. "The mystery woman in the diary must have been Esther Grey. And Zach Caulder must have been the guy she was in love with. Shouldn't we tell Mrs. Norris?"

"After the tour's over," Nancy said as George handed the framed poem back to Mrs. Norris. "I want to ask her about the donations she made on behalf of the town, too."

While the rest of their group thanked Mrs. Norris and left Esther Grey's home, Nancy, Bess, and George waited to talk to the woman. After introducing themselves to their guide, Nancy said, "We were wondering if we might ask you a few questions."

"Why, certainly," Mrs. Norris replied. Leading the way into the parlor, she gestured for the girls to sit down. When Nancy explained that they were friends of Vera's, Mrs. Norris's face brightened.

"Such a lovely woman," she said. "I'm so happy about her plans for the historical museum. I've even managed to convince Esther Grey's relatives to donate some of the poet's personal letters for the auction." She leaned forward and added confidentially, "They ought to command quite a high price."

Nancy described the poem Bess had found in Zach Caulder's diary.

"This is quite something," Mrs. Norris told them, her eyes gleaming. "Zach Caulder was indeed one

78

of the men in question, but I've never seen any kind of proof. Do you think I could see this letter and diary?"

Bess hesitated. "I'm afraid I left it back at the house," she said. "I could bring it here later, though," she offered.

"I take it you've never seen Zach Caulder's diary, then," Nancy said. Seeing Mrs. Norris's blank look, she explained, "The diary was part of the donation you made on behalf of the town for the White Falls Historical Museum."

"Oh—of course," Mrs. Norris said, nodding. "Goodness knows, I am very interested in the history of this area, but I'm afraid that, between the town council and my work here, I never did pay very close attention to those things."

She looked at the girls apologetically. "In fact, I don't think anyone had laid eyes on them in fifty years. After Zach's . . . death, when Caulder Cutlery closed . . . well, what wasn't sold was shut away in a closet in the Town Hall. I guess no one wanted to be reminded of the way Zach died."

Nancy caught Bess's meaningful glance. Mrs. Norris obviously didn't know that Esther Grey might be the person who murdered Zach. Like everyone else, she probably assumed that Charlie Shayne was responsible.

"Zach's things had been locked up there ever

79

since," Mrs. Norris went on. "After the town voted to renovate the old factory, the mayor naturally agreed to have everything sent over to Vera."

"Mrs. Norris, do you know if anyone went through the things from Caulder Cutlery before they were sent to Vera's?" Nancy asked.

"Goodness, no," the older woman answered immediately. "The dust in that closet looked as if it hadn't been disturbed in fifty years." She laughed softly and shook her head. "Vera and that boy who helped her nearly collapsed in a fit of sneezing when they came to look everything over—"

"Boy?" Nancy interrupted, leaning forward. "Did he have curly brown hair?"

Mrs. Norris nodded. "Yes, now that you mention it. And the dearest round face."

Nancy exchanged a meaningful look with Bess and George. She knew they were thinking the same thing she was.

Mike Shayne had just become their top suspect!

9

An Angry Storm

Nancy shot her friends a warning look. She couldn't wait to talk over this discovery about Mike, but she wanted to do it in private.

Rising quickly to her feet, Nancy said, "Thank you very much for your time, Mrs. Norris."

"My pleasure." Mrs. Norris stood up also and led the way to the front door. "Please don't forget to come by with that diary," she told Bess.

The girls promised Mrs. Norris they'd return as soon as possible and said goodbye.

Bess grabbed Nancy's arm as they went down the snowy front walk. "Did you hear what she said about Vera's helper?" Without waiting for an answer, she added, "Mike has to be the one who's after the money, right?"

Nancy took a few more steps down the walk before answering. "Maybe. But I'm still not convinced. If Mike stole the trunks, why did Roz try to keep George and me from looking at that black trunk we saw in her office yesterday?"

"Speaking of the black trunk," George said, "shouldn't we go back to Roz's and try to get a second look at it?"

"Definitely," Nancy told her. "But before we do that, I want to go to the newspaper office and read up on Zach Caulder's murder."

"Do you want Bess and me to go with you?" George asked as Nancy pulled the newspaper office's address from her purse.

Nancy thought for a moment. "No. Why don't you guys go back to show Mrs. Norris Zach's diary? She seems to know a lot about the area. Maybe she can tell you something that will help us figure out who might be after Zach's money chest."

The office of the *White Falls Gazette* was located in a brick building just off Main Street. Inside, a dark-haired young man behind the information desk led Nancy through the bustling newsroom to a small office at the rear of the building.

"These are the *Gazette*'s archives," he told her, gesturing around the windowless room. "We've got back issues on microfilm going back to 1898, when the paper started up."

Nancy saw that file cabinets stretched along two walls of the room, while a third wall contained shelves piled high with old copies of the *Gazette*. Next to the door was a table with two microfilm machines on it.

She remembered the date of the last entry in Zach Caulder's diary, so she asked to see the microfilm for the second half of that year.

"You're all set," the young man told her a few minutes later, after loading the microfilm. "If you'd like to make a copy of anything, just push this." He pointed to a button on the side of the machine. "Give a yell when you're done."

Once he had left, Nancy turned to the lighted monitor, and the front page of the July first issue stared back at her. She quickly ran the microfilm through until she got to August first, then checked each daily headline. She paused just long enough to make sure there was no news of Zach Caulder's murder before shooting the film ahead to the next day.

"Whoa!" she said aloud when the August sixteenth paper came up on the monitor. She did a double take when she read the large letters on the front page: Mystery Murder—Local Tycoon Found Dead.

Leaning forward, Nancy read through the article. It confirmed that Zach had been killed in his office at Caulder Cutlery and that his killer had not yet been found. In the following days the *Gazette* reported that Charlie Shayne, an employee of the factory, had been seen at Caulder Cutlery the night of the murder. A dragnet to locate him had failed, and the police assumed that Shayne had fled the area.

Since Zach had been such a prominent local figure, some of the articles speculated about his wealth. One article said that his fortune was estimated at half a million dollars.

Nancy gave a low whistle. That was a lot of money, especially fifty years ago.

Zach didn't have any living relatives, and no will, the article went on to say. Everything he owned was to be given to the state.

Nancy paused when she came across a headline that read: Caulder's Cash Missing. Apparently there were only a few hundred dollars in Zach's office safe. Not a penny more was found anywhere. The police theory was that Charlie Shayne stole the money. But Nancy knew there was another possibility: Zach Caulder's fortune might still be hidden in his secret money chest!

No mention at all was made of Esther Grey in connection to the murder, Nancy noticed. The police must have read Zach's diary during their investigation, but they didn't seem to have made a connection between Esther Grey and the love poem in the diary.

Then again, Nancy thought, that wasn't so surprising. Mrs. Norris *had* told them that Esther Grey hadn't become famous until after her death. At the time of Zach's murder, no one even knew she was a poet.

Nancy stared at the microfilm. The police must have been so convinced that Charlie was guilty that they hadn't made much of the mystery woman in Zach's diary.

Flipping back to the August sixteenth paper, Nancy glanced through all the articles a second time. One article featured a grainy photograph of Zach in his office at Caulder Cutlery. Nancy peered curiously at the heavyset man with a thick mustache who sat behind a big desk. A pocket-watch chain drooped from his vest pocket, and he smiled for the camera over wire-rimmed glasses. His desk held a carved wooden elephant, as well as an ornate clock, a box stuffed with papers, and several other items that gave the office a rich, comfortable feel.

The more Nancy looked at the photograph, the more she was struck by the odd feeling that there was something familiar about it, something she'd seen before. But she couldn't put her finger on what it could be. Nancy closed her eyes, counted to five, then looked at the photograph again. She still didn't see anything special.

It's no use, she told herself. Maybe it was just her imagination.

Nancy made copies of some of the articles, including the one with Zach's photograph. She was about to turn off the microfilm machine when a small memorial notice for Zach Caulder caught her eye. It was dated a week after the murder and printed in the *Gazette*'s old-fashioned, flowing script: "Friends and Family of Zach Caulder Mourn His Passing." Beneath it was a list of the people who had printed the notice.

Running her finger down the list, Nancy saw a lot of names she didn't recognize. She paused when she came to one that read The Grey Family. Two family members were listed in parentheses: Esther Grey and Rosalind Grey Chaplin.

"That's right!" Nancy said aloud. Mrs. Norris had mentioned that Esther Grey had a sister. And when Nancy and George had visited Roz's office, Roz mentioned having world-famous relatives. Her famous relative must have been Esther Grey.

The Roz Chaplin Nancy knew couldn't possibly be the same one as in the memorial notice, though. She was much too young to have been alive at that time. But Nancy was willing to bet that Roz's mother or grandmother was Esther Grey's sister.

And if Esther Grey had known about Zach Caulder's money, maybe her relatives knew about it, too!

* * *

"Are you trying to tell me the real reason Roz Chaplin is stealing my trunks *isn't* to wreck the crafts fair?" Vera asked at lunch that day.

"It's possible," Nancy replied. "We still don't know if Esther Grey even knew about Zach's hidden money. But if she did, her sister may have known, too. Roz could be trying to get her hands on the money Esther Grey wasn't able to find."

Vera, Nancy, Julie, Bess, and George were sitting around Vera's kitchen table, eating hot tomato soup and sandwiches. It was the first chance Nancy, Bess, and George had had to talk to Vera since they'd discovered the mention of Zach's money chest in his diary.

Julie gave Nancy a dubious look. "Don't you think you're being a little unrealistic?" she asked, picking up the second half of her sandwich. "It's obvious that Roz is stealing the trunks to try and ruin the museum project. Then Roz can go ahead with her plan to build condos on the factory site instead."

Nancy was surprised. She would have thought Julie would be glad to hear that the thief probably wasn't trying to sabotage Vera.

"The diary's pretty convincing," Bess told Julie. "I mean, Zach actually said, 'The secret of my money chest will die with me.'"

Julie shrugged. "Maybe."

Vera checked her watch. "We'd better finish eating," she said. "The crafts workshops at the old schoolhouse start in less than an hour. I told the craftspeople I'd be there to help them set up in twenty minutes."

As they all cleared the table, Julie told Vera, "I think I'll use the afternoon to catch up on the computer inventory."

"Oh, no, you won't," Vera said, wagging a finger at Julie. "This afternoon you're going to enjoy the crafts workshops. And the same goes for you three," she added to Nancy, George, and Bess. "You've all done nothing but help me for the past few days. Today I just want you to have fun."

The girls looked at each other and laughed. "I think we can follow that order without any problem at all," Nancy told Vera.

It wasn't until they were all piled into Vera's van and on their way to the old schoolhouse that Nancy remembered to ask Bess and George, "By the way, did you learn anything else from Mrs. Norris when you showed her Zach Caulder's diary?"

George rolled her eyes. "Miss Elephant's Memory here suddenly couldn't remember where she left the diary, so we couldn't show it to anyone."

"Including me," Vera put in. Grinning at Nancy, she said, "I was really looking forward to reading the juicy parts."

"I feel awful," Bess wailed. "I was sure I left it by my bed, but it's not there now."

Nancy punched Bess lightly on the arm. "Well, it's not worth feeling miserable about. I'm sure we'll find it somewhere when we get back tonight."

They pulled up in front of a one-story wooden building a few minutes later. Julie had driven her own car. She was waiting outside the schoolhouse with a few people who were ready to set up their workshops.

When they went inside Nancy saw that the building was really one long room. A line of windows ran down both sides, and a sloping ceiling rose sharply to a point overhead. The room had been divided into sections, and brightly colored banners hung from the solid wooden beams, announcing each workshop.

As the craftsmen set up their areas, the school was quickly filled with a weaving loom, a woodworker's bench, and a patchwork cover being stretched in a frame for quilting. Outside the schoolhouse, a glassblower and a man who made cast-iron weather vanes were also setting up shop.

Half an hour later, the schoolhouse was crowded with tourists and townspeople trying their hands at the various crafts. Nancy had just finished weaving a small star pattern when she saw Grace Shayne enter the schoolhouse. The woman was wearing a brown pantsuit, and her hair was pulled back into its severe bun.

Nancy realized that this was her chance to find out if Mike had alibis for the times when the two trunks were stolen. Leaving the weaving workshop, Nancy followed Grace Shayne over to the quilting workshop. Before Mike's aunt could sit down and take up a needle, Nancy hurried to her side and said hello.

"I was wondering if I could ask you some more questions about Mike, Mrs. Shayne?" Nancy asked. Seeing Mrs. Shayne glance at the quilting frame, she added, "It'll only take a minute."

"Well, all right," Mrs. Shayne said with a tight smile.

Nancy led Mike's aunt to a corner near the door that wasn't too crowded. The first thing she wanted to find out was whether Mike had alibis for the times when the two trunks were stolen. But when Nancy asked Mrs. Shayne where Mike had been on those occasions, the woman pressed her lips together.

"The only times Mike comes home these days is to eat and to sleep," Mrs. Shayne said. "Where he is the rest of the time is a mystery to me."

"I see," Nancy said. "Do you know if he's friends with any older kids, boys or girls who have their driver's licenses?" If he did, that might explain how he'd managed to move the stolen trunks.

Mrs. Shayne thought for a moment, then shook her head. "Not that I know of."

Nancy was about to ask Mrs. Shayne more about Charlie's involvement with Zach Caulder's murder when a commotion near the door drew her attention.

Roz Chaplin was standing in front of Vera. Her face had turned an angry red that matched her hair, and her jaw was tightly clenched. "This time you've gone too far, Vera Alexander," Roz shrieked.

"*You're* the one who's going too far," Vera snapped back, planting her hands on her hips. "But at least this time you decided to face me directly instead of sneaking around behind my back."

Nancy watched the angry exchange in surprise. What was Roz talking about? Neither Roz nor Vera seemed to notice that people at the nearby workshops had paused to stare at them.

The color in Roz's face deepened to a mottled purple. "I don't have to take this from you," she sputtered. "I know what you've done, and believe me, you're not going to get away with it." She pointed a long, manicured finger at Vera. "If you cross me again, I'll make sure you regret it!"

10

Emergency Sleuthing

With a final scathing look at Vera, Roz turned on her heel and stormed out of the schoolhouse.

Nancy quickly excused herself from Mrs. Shayne and hurried over to Vera. "What was that all about?" Nancy asked.

"Who knows?" Vera said, throwing up her hands. "Ooh, she makes me so mad," she went on, her dark eyes flashing. "That woman has some nerve threatening me like that, after all she's done to try to ruin me."

Looking around them, Nancy realized with a start that the people at the workshops were still staring at Vera. A few people were actually gathering their things, as if they were about to leave.

"Everything's fine, folks," Vera announced. She

forced a smile and stepped over to the group of quilters. "Please, just continue with what you were doing."

As the hum of activity slowly started up again, Vera walked back to Nancy, followed immediately by Julie.

"I knew Roz Chaplin was trouble," Julie said, looking very angry. "Don't you think this proves she really is trying to sabotage us?"

"I'm not sure *what* this proves," Nancy said, frowning. "But I think it's time I paid Roz Chaplin another visit. Vera, could I borrow your van?"

Vera looked as if she was about to object. "I wanted you girls to enjoy yourselves today, remember?" she began. But then she let out a resigned sigh and handed Nancy the keys. "Just promise me you'll be careful, Nancy."

Scanning the crowded schoolhouse, Nancy spotted George at the woodworking workshop. Nancy made her way through the crowd to her friend, who was watching a young carpenter carve a design of leaves and grapes into a kitchen cabinet door.

"We've got an emergency," Nancy whispered. She pulled George away from the group and told her about Roz's threat.

"I don't get it," George said, crinkling up her nose. "What do you think Roz meant when she said she knows what Vera's done?"

Nancy shrugged. "I'm not sure, but I don't think

93

we can afford to wait around and find out. The auction is tomorrow. If Roz is planning something to ruin it, I think we should try to find out how and stop her. Besides, I want to see if that black lacquered trunk is still there. Have you seen Bess?"

"I think she said something about checking out the glassblowing workshop outside," George told her.

Saying goodbye to Vera and Julie, the two girls grabbed their jackets and left the schoolhouse. To the right of the door, a woman wearing overalls, gloves, and protective goggles was blowing a blob of hot melted glass into an ornament.

Bess was standing at the front of the group of people crowded around the woman. George managed to catch her cousin's eye and gesture for her to join them.

"Sorry to drag you away, Bess, but we've got to make an emergency trip to Roz Chaplin's office," Nancy said when Bess came over.

Bess nodded. "I saw her storm in and out a couple of minutes ago. Boy, did she look angry." Then Bess's eyes widened. "Oh, no! Did she do anything to Vera?"

George shook her head. "Not yet, but she might be planning to," she said grimly. "Come on. We'll explain on the way."

A few minutes later, the girls were driving Vera's

van down Main Street toward the edge of White Falls.

"So what's our plan, Nancy?" Bess asked after George and Nancy had told her about Roz's threat.

"Well, Roz already knows George and me," she said slowly. "She'll be too suspicious if we show up."

"So that leaves me, right?" Bess asked, grinning.

"Right." Nancy glanced at Bess's reflection in the rearview mirror. "I think you're about to be struck by an irresistible urge to redo your condominium in a more modern style."

Bess giggled. "But I don't even own a condo," she objected.

Nancy nodded. "You know that, and George and I know that . . ."

The three girls broke into laughter, finishing the thought at the same time. "But Roz Chaplin doesn't!"

When the girls reached the little mall where Roz's real estate development office was located, Nancy parked the van at the very edge of the parking lot, next to a snowdrift. She hoped the van wouldn't be too noticeable from Roz's office. Then she and George waited in the van while Bess walked to the office and went inside.

"Great. Roz just took Bess into her inside office,"

Nancy said a few minutes later. She stopped peering through the front windshield and turned to George. "Let's go."

Getting out of the van, she and George skirted around the corner of the mall and headed toward the side garage entrance they had seen during their earlier visit.

George frowned as they reached the corrugated-steel gate that was closed over the garage opening. "If we try to open this thing, it'll make too much noise. Someone's bound to hear us. How are we going to get inside?"

Nancy scrutinized the outside wall. "Over there," she said finally, pointing to a small opening in the cinder-block wall beyond the gate. Hurrying over to the opening, Nancy found a reinforced steel door. She tried to turn the knob, but the door was locked.

"No problem," she murmured, reaching for the lock-picking set she always carried with her. After a few tries, the lock clicked open.

Nancy held her breath and pulled the door open a crack. "We're in luck," she whispered to George. "It looks empty."

The two girls stepped inside quickly and silently. The windowless space was almost completely dark, except for a small sliver of light that seeped under the corrugated gate. Nancy heard a *thunk* and a muffled "Ouch!" as George bumped into something. Pausing, Nancy reached into her purse for her penlight and shone the beam into the darkness.

Picking their way around the furniture, carpet rolls, and paint samples, the two girls made their way over to the crates behind which they had seen the black lacquered trunk. But when Nancy flashed her beam over the area, she saw only the crates and the bare concrete floor.

"We should have known," George said with a groan. "Roz moved the trunk already."

"There are still plenty of places out here where it could be," Nancy said. "We'll just have to look a little harder, that's all."

As Nancy shone her penlight around the garage, George pointed to a lumpy tarp in the corner, beyond the door that led to the office. "I don't remember that being here, do you, Nan?"

Nancy hurried over to the tarp, lifted it up, and peeked underneath it.

"Bingo!" she said softly.

There, sitting side by side on the garage floor, were the wooden captain's trunk Nancy recognized from Vera's workroom and the black lacquered trunk she and George had spotted in the garage earlier.

"Is there any yellow paint on that black one?" George asked, coming up beside Nancy.

Nancy was already on her knees. She shone her penlight carefully over the lacquered chest, stopping at the back left corner. Sure enough, the penlight's beam shone on a splintered dent that was marked by a bright yellow gash of paint.

"Well, we have our proof," Nancy said, standing up again. "I think we can call the police now. They'll make sure Roz doesn't cause any more trouble."

She was about to open the trunks when a rattling at the inside door made her whirl around. Nancy dropped the tarp quickly back over the trunks again, just as the door was flung open.

"Oh, no, I really don't need to see anything right now," Bess said in a frantic voice.

"Nonsense," Roz interrupted. "Once you see this chair, I'm sure you'll agree it's exactly what you're looking for."

The lights blinked on, flooding the garage in bright white fluorescence. There was no time to move or hide. Nancy had a sinking feeling in the pit of her stomach as Roz stepped into the garage. When the real estate developer's gaze landed on Nancy and George, she stopped in her tracks and her mouth fell open.

11

Roz's Story

If looks could kill, Nancy thought, George and I would be dead right now.

Roz stalked over to where Nancy and George were standing, next to the trunks. Behind Roz, Bess threw her hands in a helpless gesture. "Sorry," she mouthed.

"I've had it up to here with your tricks," Roz snapped. Her gaze shot quickly from Nancy and George to Bess. Then comprehension dawned in her hazel eyes.

"You're with them, aren't you?" she asked Bess. The words came out sounding more like an accusation than a question. "Well, I've got news for all of you. You're trespassing, and I'm going to call the police right now."

"Go right ahead," Nancy said, squarely facing Roz. "In fact, I'd like to talk to them, too. I think the police will be very interested to know you're the person who's been sabotaging Vera."

Roz looked nervously at the garage's cement floor. "I don't know what you're talking about," she said.

"You don't?" George asked. "Well, maybe we can refresh your memory." Lifting the tarp, she revealed the two trunks. "Once we tell the police about these, they'll make sure you don't ever bother Vera Alexander again."

Nancy expected to see a nervous reaction from Roz, but instead the woman looked angrier than ever. "Vera put you up to this," she sputtered. "You girls put those trunks here yourselves to set me up! What else were you going to plant in my garage?"

What's going on here? Nancy wondered. Roz was hardly acting like a woman who'd been caught red-handed.

"Are you trying to say you didn't steal these trunks from Vera?" Nancy asked, eyeing Roz skeptically. "You think *we* put them here?"

"Give us a break," Bess muttered.

Roz wagged a finger at the girls. "Don't try that innocent act with me."

"I suppose you think we're the ones who pushed that bale of hay at Vera, too," George spoke up.

"That had nothing to do with these trunks—"

Roz broke off, clamping her mouth shut as she realized her slip. Taking a deep breath, she looked nervously around the garage. Then she turned back to the girls. "All right," she said, "I think you all had better come inside so we can talk."

Nancy, Bess, and George followed Roz inside to her office. Under the desk, Fifi was curled up in a padded wicker basket, her front paws draped protectively over a rubber bone. Nancy wasn't sure what was going on, so she decided to just listen to what Roz had to say.

Roz let out a sigh as she motioned for the girls to sit down. "Fifi was the reason I went up into the loft at the barn dance," she began. The developer reached down from her desk chair, picked up the fluffy white dog, and settled it in her lap. "She had gotten hold of that boy's harmonica and brought it up there. Well, naturally I couldn't let her play in all that filthy straw."

Out of the corner of her eye, Nancy saw George roll her eyes.

"Anyway, I had just managed to get the harmonica away from Fifi when I slipped in that awful hay. That's when the bale fell over the edge of the loft." The annoyance in her voice was clear as she added, "My new heels were *ruined.*"

"Who cares about a dumb pair of shoes?" Bess said indignantly. "Vera could have been hurt."

"I'm telling you, it was an accident," Roz insisted. "I knew no one would believe me, though. Everyone knows that Vera is not exactly my favorite person in White Falls. That's why I sneaked down the outside ladder and didn't say anything."

Nancy looked critically at Roz. The woman sounded sincere, but Nancy wasn't sure whether to believe her. "What about the trunks?" she prodded.

Roz sighed. "The first time I saw the black one was when Fifi pulled that quilt from it the other day. As for the second trunk, I found it in the garage this morning." Angry sparks flashed in her eyes. "I knew Vera had to be the one who put them there, to make me look bad."

"So that's why you went to the crafts workshops, to yell at Vera because you thought she set you up," Nancy guessed.

"She *did* set me up," Roz said. "Face it, girls. If I had stolen those trunks, I would hardly draw attention to myself by confronting Vera. Especially not in front of dozens of potential real estate customers."

Nancy was beginning to get the feeling that Roz was telling the truth—about the trunks, anyway. She *had* acted surprised when she'd first seen the lacquered chest the other day. And so far, there was no indication that Roz even knew those two trunks had belonged to Zach Caulder. Besides, even if she knew about the secret money chest, how would she know to steal those particular trunks?

It was time to find out what, if anything, Roz knew about Zach Caulder's hidden money. "Is it true that the poet Esther Grey was a relative of yours?" Nancy asked.

Roz looked confused by this sudden change of questioning. "Why, yes, it is. Esther Grey was my mother's sister," she said proudly.

"We took a tour of her house today," George told Roz. "We couldn't help wondering if Esther was really in love with a mystery man?"

"You know," Bess added quickly, "someone like Zach Caulder?"

Roz waved a hand dismissively. "I wish you people would stop coming up with these crazy theories," she said. "The only man my aunt was in love with was an imaginary one she wrote poems about." She gave the girls a knowing look. "If Esther had really been in love, I'm sure my mother would have told me about it."

"So you don't think it could have been Zach Caulder?" Bess pressed. She gave Nancy a secret wink. "I mean, with all the money he had, Zach would have been quite a catch."

Roz snorted derisively. "Money? Hah! When Zach died, he didn't even have enough cash to pay his workers their last week's salary."

"Surely he had more money in the bank, or stashed away somewhere," Nancy said.

"Well, if he did, that's news to me and to everyone else," Roz said.

Nancy watched Roz's face carefully, but the real estate developer didn't seem to know anything about any hidden money.

After asking a few more roundabout questions, Nancy, Bess, and George rose to leave.

"I hope you'll be taking those moldy trunks with you," Roz said. "I don't want them in my garage for another second."

The girls quickly said goodbye and carted the two trunks out to Vera's minivan. The sun had sunk low in the sky, and ribbons of deep orange and red wove along the western horizon.

Nancy stepped into the van's dim interior. "Whoever took the trunks probably already checked for a hidden compartment, but I think we should, too," she told Bess and George.

She knelt down on the van's floor next to the wooden chest. Opening the lid, she peered inside. "We should look for any difference between the outside and inside dimensions. That could indicate a secret compartment. Also, if the wood doesn't sound solid, there could be a hidden hollow area."

Bess tapped on the trunk's lid. "That sounds pretty solid," she said. Her breath made puffy clouds in the cold wintry air.

First the girls emptied the trunks of the quilts and vintage clothing stored inside them. Using

Nancy's penlight, they examined first the wooden trunk, then the black lacquered one.

"Nothing," George announced several minutes later. She closed the lid of the lacquered chest and sat back on her heels.

With a sigh, Nancy clicked off her penlight and climbed into the driver's seat. "Since we didn't find a compartment, at least we can be pretty sure that whoever stole the trunks hasn't found Zach's money yet."

"So what do we do now?" Bess asked.

"I'm not sure," Nancy admitted. "For now, I guess we'd better get back to the crafts workshops. Vera must be wondering where we are."

Pulling the van's keys from her purse, Nancy revved the motor, then pulled the van back toward town. They drove in silence for a while.

"It looks like the weather will be good for tomorrow's auction," Bess commented, staring out the passenger window. "It's a beautiful night."

Moonlight shimmered on the river, casting a silvery luster over the trees on the opposite side of the river.

Suddenly George gasped. "Hey, look at Caulder Cutlery!"

"What is it?" Quickly pulling the van over to the curb, Nancy took a second look across the river. She could just make out the shadowy outline of the old factory, with spots of moonlight glinting off the ivy.

Most of the factory was a solid black silhouette, but Nancy saw a light flickering in one of the lower windows.

"It looks like a candle," she said slowly. She blinked and looked again, but the light was still there. Someone was in the factory!

12

A Mysterious Light

"Do you think it's someone looking for Zach's money chest?" Bess asked excitedly.

"There's only one way to find out," Nancy replied. "Hold on to your hats, guys!"

Nancy pulled the van around in a screeching U-turn and headed back the short distance to the bridge.

"It might not be anything weird," George said, grabbing her seat as a bump in the bridge sent her bouncing. "I mean, maybe it's just Julie or Vera, doing something for the museum."

"In the dark? I doubt it," Nancy replied. "Besides, with all they had to do for the crafts workshops today, I don't think they'd be over at the factory now."

Nancy turned right on the road they had taken from the factory the day before. Two minutes later they reached the drive to Caulder Cutlery, and Nancy pulled the van to a halt.

When the girls got out of the van, the snow crunched under their feet, disturbing the eerie quiet. A faint wind whistled through the tree branches and ruffled the ivy covering the building, but otherwise there wasn't a single noise.

"It looks totally dark in there," Bess whispered, peering uncertainly at the deep shadows enveloping Caulder Cutlery. "Are you sure it's okay to go inside? Maybe we should wait until morning."

George shook her head. "No way," she said. "Someone's in there, and we need to find out who it is."

Nancy nodded. "The light we saw was on the lower level, facing the river. That's why we can't see it from here."

She headed toward the factory's front entrance, her boots crunching on the snow. But when she tried the front door, it wouldn't budge. "It's locked," she called back softly to Bess and George.

"So it's definitely not Vera or Julie," Bess put in nervously. "They'd use a key."

"Let's go around to the side, the way Mike and I got in yesterday," Nancy suggested. "Julie said she was going to nail it shut, but whoever's in there had to have gotten in somehow."

"It's worth a try," George said as she and Bess fell into step behind Nancy.

The noise of their footsteps sounded loud to Nancy as they plodded through the snow to the side window. "Be really quiet when we go inside," she whispered to her friends. "We don't want to give the person a chance to get away."

The three-quarter moon was bright enough for Nancy to see the matted-down spot in the snow to which she'd followed Mike the day before. Within seconds she found the window beneath the ivy. She pushed against the window frame, and it opened easily inward.

Behind her, George whispered, "It's a good thing for us Julie forgot to secure this window."

"Well, here goes nothing," Nancy said. She pulled herself up and through the window, landing lightly on the wooden floor of the factory's main level. A moment later, Bess and George were next to her.

"What are you looking at, Nancy?" Bess whispered as Nancy bent over a shadowy lump on the floor.

Pulling out her penlight, Nancy shone it over two pieces of wood. Each of them was about two feet long. Nails were stuck through both ends of the boards, as if they had once been attached to something else.

"That's funny," Nancy murmured. "These

109

weren't here yesterday." She stood up and used her penlight to illuminate the inside of the window frame. There, next to the lower corners of the window, were several nail holes.

"It looks like Julie did block this window," Nancy said softly, running her fingers over the holes. "She nailed the boards diagonally over the bottom corners so that the window couldn't be pushed in."

"That means someone would have to take the boards down from the inside," George whispered. Nancy couldn't see her friend clearly in the dark factory, but she heard a puzzled tone in her voice. "I don't get it. If the place was locked up, how could anyone get inside in the first place to loosen the boards?"

Nancy peered into the inky blackness, trying to make out the staircase against the far wall. "Maybe whoever's down in the basement can tell us the answer to that question," she said.

Shining her penlight on the wooden floor, Nancy led the way across the main level, stopping at the top of the staircase. She still didn't see any light. With a quick glance at her friends, Nancy held a finger to her lip, then tentatively lowered her foot to the first step.

As silently as they could, the girls made their way downward. When Nancy rounded the corner of the stairwell, she paused. Still no light. Frowning, she shone her penlight into the basement. There was nothing there except the bare shelves she'd glimpsed during her earlier visit.

"It's empty," Bess murmured in disbelief, her voice echoing in the deserted room. "How could the person have gotten away without us even seeing or hearing anything?"

Nancy, Bess, and George descended the last few steps, being careful to avoid the caved-in bottom step Nancy had fallen on the day before. Nancy felt a bubble of frustration building inside her. She'd been sure someone was here. Even now, the feeling was so strong, she couldn't believe the room was empty.

Cautiously she began circling the basement, shining her penlight over every inch of it. "We know someone *was* here just a minute ago," she murmured, thinking out loud. "So there must be at least some clue—a candle, or a match . . . something."

"That's right. The light looked kind of like a candle flame from across the river," George said. She wrinkled up her nose as she sniffed the air. "But there isn't even the smell of a burned match."

Nancy played the bright beam over each of the three windowsills. Nothing was adding up, she thought, frowning.

"Hey, I just remembered something," Bess said. "Remember when we stopped on the bridge yesterday to look at the factory?"

George sighed. "You mean, when you were going totally crazy about Zach Caulder's diary?" she asked. "Bess, this is no time to get sentimental."

"No. That's not what I meant. What I was going to say was I thought there were four windows on the lower level of this factory, not three."

"That's right!" Nancy exclaimed. "Bess, you're a genius."

George was walking toward the wall farthest from the staircase. "You know, this room doesn't seem as long as the main floor upstairs, either," she said, picking up on her cousin's thought.

Nancy rushed over to join George. "There has to be another room. But how do we get to it?"

Using her penlight, Nancy began examining the wall, which was covered with rows of shelves that ran from floor to ceiling. Each row was about three feet wide and separated from the next row by a vertical support.

"Doesn't this row of shelves look a little narrower than the others?" Nancy asked, heading toward the row farthest from the windows.

"You're right!" George replied.

Nancy ran her fingers along the support board. As she did so, the shelves swiveled like a revolving door, revealing another room.

At first, all Nancy saw was the flickering orange glow from a candle flame. Then she made out the rumpled cushions and blankets in the corner of the room that looked like a makeshift bed.

Her heart racing, Nancy squeezed by the shelves and into the room. Bess and George were right behind her. Before them, leaning against the wall, was Mike Shayne, his face frozen in shock.

"Mike! What are you—?"

Nancy's voice broke off as she realized that Mike was not alone. Beside him, on a rickety wooden chair, was a much older man. He wore faded blue jeans, worn leather work boots, and a red long-sleeved undershirt that looked as if it hadn't been washed in weeks. Beneath his thick gray hair and grizzled beard, his round face looked strikingly like Mike's. Despite his unkempt appearance, Nancy saw that the look in the old man's brown eyes was gentle and kind.

"And who might you be, miss?" the old man asked in a gravelly voice.

Mike took a step away from the wall. "She's the one I told you about, Grandpa," he said. "Vera's nosy friend."

Nancy started at Mike's words. "Grandpa?" she echoed, staring at the old man in disbelief. "But that means you're . . ."

The man nodded, a slight smile curving his lips. "Charlie Shayne, at your service."

13

Old Stories

For a long moment, all Nancy could do was stare at Charlie Shayne. The man who had been accused of killing Zach Caulder was standing right in front of her.

"What are you doing here?" Bess asked, sounding flabbergasted. "Everyone said you left town right after you murdered—" She broke off with a gasp, and her hands flew to her mouth. "Oh," she said.

Mike's grandfather merely crossed his arms over his chest, an amused look on his wrinkled features. "Well now, young lady. Did it ever occur to you that maybe not everyone around here knows what they're talkin' about?"

Was he trying to tell them that he hadn't killed

Zach Caulder? Nancy wondered. And if so, should they believe him?

"Mr. Shayne, um, what exactly *are* you doing here?" Nancy asked.

"You don't have to say anything, Grandpa," Mike said quickly. He stuffed his hands into his pockets and shot the girls an angry glare.

"I don't guess it's any of your business," Charlie said, rubbing his head.

"Sabotaging our friend's museum is definitely our business," George said angrily.

Charlie chuckled deeply, waving a wrinkled hand around the dank, bare room. "Museum? Oh, yes, this is quite a palace." He was still looking at them with the same amused expression.

"Go ahead and laugh," Nancy told the old man, "but Mike's already in a lot of trouble for throwing that rusty bin at me yesterday."

Mike glanced fearfully at Nancy. Then he blurted out, "I didn't mean to hurt you. Honest. I was just afraid you were going to find Grandpa."

Nancy nodded. Suddenly things were beginning to fall into place in her mind. "That's why you made those phone calls to Vera, too, telling her to stay away from Caulder Cutlery," she guessed. "And the money you stole from Vera—was it to take care of your grandfather?"

Mike shuffled his feet and nodded. "Grandpa didn't even tell Aunt Grace and Uncle Phil he was

115

back. He knew Aunt Grace would go right to the police. She hates him." Looking at Nancy, he added, "I only took a little money. Just enough to buy Grandpa some stuff to eat."

Nancy turned to Charlie and frowned. "If you really want us to believe you, you're going to have to tell us what happened the night Zach Caulder was murdered."

"Was it Esther Grey?" Bess asked in an excited whisper. "Did *she* do it?"

Charlie glared at Bess. "Don't you dare speak of Esther that way!"

Then, for a long moment, he was silent. A faraway look came into his eyes. "She was quite a lady, Esther was," Charlie went on in a softer, dreamy tone. "Not that she ever knew I carried a torch for her, mind you. She probably didn't even know I was alive. I wouldn't have expected a lady like her to have anything to do with a simple factory worker like me."

"Grandpa, don't say that," Mike said quickly.

But Charlie was so lost in his memories that he didn't appear to have heard his grandson. "My wife had passed on, you see, and I thought it would be best for my son, Phil, to stay with my sister and her kids. So I was all alone, just like Esther. I made it my business to keep an eye out for her. She needed someone to take care of her."

The old man shook his head sadly. "I never did

116

understand what it was she saw in a cold fish like Zach Caulder."

Nancy exchanged excited looks with Bess and George. So Esther Grey *was* Zach's mystery woman!

After a long pause, Charlie went on, "I don't think anyone but me noticed that she was leaving him things . . . flowers, notes. It just about broke my heart to see her pouring her love out that way when there was no chance he would ever return it."

"How sad," Bess murmured.

"Yes, ma'am, it was," Charlie agreed with a nod. Then his expression hardened. "All that heart wasted on a mean old miser."

As Nancy listened, she was struck by the sudden bitterness in Charlie's voice. Could he have been so jealous of Zach that he'd murdered him? "It must have made you furious to see the way Zach ignored Esther," she said, choosing her words carefully.

"He wasn't good enough for Esther, not by a long shot," Charlie declared angrily.

As gently as she could, Nancy said, "And that's why you killed Zach Caulder, wasn't it? To protect Esther from him, I mean."

"Grandpa didn't kill anyone," Mike said, stepping defensively in front of Charlie. "That poet lady did it!"

Charlie turned sharply toward his grandson, but Mike cried, "No, Grandpa, I won't stay quiet!" He whirled toward Nancy, an earnest look on his round

117

face. "Grandpa made me promise not to tell any-one, but I won't let everyone think he killed some-one when he didn't!"

"Wow," Bess whispered. "I don't believe I'm hearing this."

Nancy could hardly believe it, either. "Maybe you'd like to tell us what really happened, Mr. Shayne," she said carefully.

During Mike's outburst, Charlie had been sitting with his head in his hands. Finally he stroked his gray beard and sighed.

"I guess it can't do any harm to tell the truth," he said slowly. "Esther's been gone so long, I don't suppose she can be hurt by it now. Besides, I'm an old man." Charlie looked at Mike and clapped a wrinkled, callused hand on the boy's shoulder. "I've come back to White Falls to spend some time with my grandson. It's time to make peace with my family."

"What really happened the night Zach was mur-dered?" Bess asked.

Charlie leveled a long look at the girls. "I was there when it happened," he said at last. "But I didn't kill Zach Caulder.

"Evenings was usually when Esther would sneak up to leave things for Zach. As I said, I liked to look out for her, so I used to stay late at the factory on purpose. I was the last one to leave that night, except for Mr. Caulder. I remember being sur-

118

prised that Esther actually went into the building, instead of just leaving a secret something in Zach's car, the way she usually did."

"So he never knew who was leaving him the things?" George asked softly.

Charlie nodded. "I'm sure Esther thought no one ever saw her—Zach or me or anyone else. That night she was a scary sight. She had a crazy look on her face, like she was going to do something drastic, so I followed her. I waited downstairs, but I could hear what they said."

Nancy felt as if she were listening to a history book come alive. She didn't dare say anything that would break the old man's reminiscence. In the flickering glow from the candle, she saw that everyone else seemed mesmerized, too.

"It was the first time she'd ever actually faced him in person," Charlie went on. "Esther came right out and told Mr. Caulder she loved him and wanted to marry him, and he had the nerve to laugh in her face." Charlie's voice was filled with outrage. "He accused her of being a fortune hunter."

George shook her head. "I knew he was a jerk," she said disgustedly.

Charlie nodded his agreement. "I guess even Mr. Caulder didn't deserve to go the way he did, though. The scream he let out after that chilled me to the bone. I just knew Esther had done something awful. Before I could even run up to Mr. Caulder's

119

office, Esther came out. The way she moved down the stairs, it was like she was in a trance. As soon as I saw the knife in her hand, I knew she'd killed him. . . ."

Bess gasped. "Please, I think I've heard enough," she said in a high, squeaky voice.

"Mr. Shayne, why did you let everyone believe *you* had killed Zach Caulder?" Nancy asked.

"Esther was in shock," Charlie said. "She didn't recognize me, didn't hardly know I was there. I had the feeling she didn't really understand what she'd done." The same sad, faraway look returned to his eyes. "I couldn't bear the thought of her being sent to jail."

"So you hid the knife," Nancy guessed.

Charlie nodded. "Took it away from her and threw it in the river. Then I took Esther to her house. Afterward, I went back to the factory, just to make sure there wasn't anything else Esther had left behind. Good thing I did, too."

"Why is that?" Bess asked.

"All those letters Esther had written to Mr. Caulder," Charlie replied. "They were in a box on Mr. Caulder's office desk. If the police had found them, they might have made the connection with Esther. I couldn't let that happen, so I took the letters and brought them back to Esther."

Charlie paused, staring briefly at the candle flame. "Anyway, someone must have seen me when

I went back to the factory. The next thing I knew, the papers were saying I was a murderer. That's when I had to leave White Falls. So I went to Canada. Stayed there until about two weeks ago." With a fond look at Mike, Charlie added, "Like I said, I want to be with my family."

Nancy was glad Mike and his grandfather were reunited. But he still hadn't said anything about Zach's money. "You didn't take anything else from the office?" Nancy asked.

A glint of amusement came back into Charlie's eyes. "Now, what else would there be to take?" he asked. "It's not like old Mr. Caulder left all his money sitting out for me to grab or anything."

As Charlie laughed quietly to himself, Nancy looked him over critically. In his ragged old clothes, Charlie looked as if he'd never had very much money—certainly not half a million dollars. But, except when he talked about Esther Grey, he was acting as if everything was a big joke.

Nancy didn't know whether to take him seriously. Maybe he really had stolen the money. The question was, how could she find out for sure?

"I can't believe Charlie Shayne came back to White Falls after all these years," Julie Bergson said the next morning, shaking her head in amazement.

She had arrived at Vera's to find Vera, Bess, Nancy, and George sitting around the kitchen table, their plates piled high with buttermilk pancakes. The story of the girls' encounter with Charlie and Mike had come spilling out as Vera set an extra plate on the table for Julie.

"I contacted Mike's family as soon as the girls told me the story," Vera told her excitedly. "Phil Shayne was so pleased with the news about his father. He said he wants Charlie to live with them, but it's going to take a few days to get Grace used to the idea."

"And until then, Vera said Charlie could stay on at the factory," Bess added. "He doesn't seem to have done any harm there." She reached for three more pancakes from the tray and lathered them with butter and maple syrup from the crafts fair maple boil.

Vera shook her head. "This is so exciting."

"What about Zach's money?" Julie asked. "Did Charlie say anything about that?" She grinned. "I mean, not that I believe that old story, but it's incredible that he's back in White Falls again."

Nancy tuned out the conversation as Bess and George described the conversation with Charlie. In her mind, she kept going over and over the pieces of the puzzle that still didn't fit.

There was Charlie's cryptic statement about the money. Nancy didn't quite trust him, but she didn't see how he and Mike could have moved the two trunks around, either, since they didn't seem to have a car. Her instincts told her that Roz had been telling the truth about being set up, too. Even if the real estate broker had knocked over that bale of hay, it looked as if she wasn't the thief.

Nancy sighed in frustration. So who had stolen the trunks? And where was the money hidden? The auction was to begin in a few hours, and she was no closer to solving the case than she'd been when she first arrived in White Falls.

"Nancy, did you hear what Julie just said?"

Bess's question cut into Nancy's thoughts. Looking up with a start, Nancy realized that everyone was staring at her. She smiled sheepishly. "Sorry, I was thinking about the case. What did you say, Julie?"

"I asked whether you've found out who's trying to steal the money," Julie repeated. She looked expectantly at Nancy.

Nancy shook her head. "I just can't figure it out," she said. "I know I'm missing something that's right in front of me. It's driving me crazy."

Getting up from the table, Nancy excused herself and went into the living room. She returned a moment later with the photocopies she'd made at the *White Falls Gazette* office.

"Every time I look at these, I get a really strong feeling that the key to this case is somewhere in these articles."

Holding on to the article with the photograph of

123

Zach Caulder in his office, Nancy plunked the remaining copies down on the table. Julie reached over and began flipping eagerly through them. Vera, Bess, and George leaned over the table so they could look, too.

For the zillionth time, Nancy stared at the grainy photograph, taking in every detail. Her eyes roved over the picture on the office wall, the desk clock, the box of letters . . .

Suddenly Nancy's breath caught in her throat. She turned to her friends, a triumphant look on her face. "You guys, I think I just figured out where Zach Caulder's money is!"

14

The Secret of the Money Chest

Everyone looked stunned at Nancy's announcement.

Nancy pointed excitedly to the picture of Zach Caulder's office, touching the image of a carved box on his desk. The box looked about ten inches deep and a foot and a half long.

"I knew there was something familiar about this photograph. See that carved box on his desk? We saw it yesterday. . . ."

Bess gasped as she looked at the picture. "It was in Esther Grey's house!" she exclaimed. "The box of letters in her study!"

"Charlie said he took a bunch of Esther Grey's letters back to her house after the murder," George remembered. "He must have taken the chest they were in, too."

As Nancy put the picture down on the table, Julie leaned over to look at it. " 'If need be, the secret of my money chest will die with me,' " Julie murmured dreamily. "Isn't that what Zach wrote? Whoever would have thought the box would be so small?"

"I know what you mean," Bess said. "It never even occurred to me that his money chest would be small enough to fit on a desk."

Julie seemed to shake herself out of her daydream and stood up. She looked quickly around the table. "Well, there are some last-minute items that still need to be delivered to the White Falls Inn for the auction," she said. "I guess I'll start loading them up."

"I can't believe that there might be a half a million dollars sitting in Esther Grey's house right now," Vera said. She shook her head. "I'm afraid the Esther Grey House is closed today, though. We'll have to wait until tomorrow to examine the chest."

"It's been sitting there for over fifty years," George said with a shrug. "I guess another day can't hurt."

As Julie disappeared out the kitchen door with an armful of things, Vera looked after her distractedly. "I think I'd better help load up the van," Vera said. She pushed her chair back and stood up. "If I don't start moving, I'll just sit here in shock all day long."

Nancy, Bess, and George cleared the table. "It's too bad we still don't know who's after the money," Nancy said, filling the sink with hot, soapy water.

"I wish there was some way we could get a look at that box before tomorrow," Bess said. She picked up a towel and began wiping the dishes after they had been washed and rinsed. "I don't think I can stand waiting a whole day to find out if you're right, Nancy."

"Why don't we call Mrs. Norris?" George suggested.

She went over to the edge of the counter, where a phone sat on top of a yellow directory. "Norris, Norris," George murmured, flipping through the pages. "Here it is." She looked expectantly at Nancy and Bess. "Should I call her?"

"Don't even ask, George," Bess said. "Just dial."

George gave Nancy and Bess a thumbs-up sign a few moments later as she said hello into the receiver and told Mrs. Norris who she was.

"That's right," George said. "My friends and I are the ones with the diary. . . . No, I'm sorry, we haven't been able to locate it yet, but we did find out something else that could be very important."

In all the excitement of figuring out where the money chest was, Nancy had completely forgotten about the diary. Bess had still been searching for the old leather volume the night before when Nancy went to sleep.

"You didn't find it yet?" she asked Bess now, speaking in a low tone so as not to distract George.

Bess shook her head. "I've looked *everywhere.*"

"Well, we'd rather talk to you about it in person," George was saying to Mrs. Norris. "Do you think we could meet you at Esther Grey's home today? . . . Yes, we're going to be at the auction, too. How about after it's over?"

For a long time George didn't say anything, and Nancy was afraid Mrs. Norris was telling her no. Then George smiled broadly. "Thank you very much, Mrs. Norris," she said into the receiver. "We'll see you at the auction. 'Bye."

"She said yes!" George cried, hanging up. "We're supposed to meet her after the auction. Then we'll all go over to Esther Grey's house together." She giggled. "Mrs. Norris told me she said yes because she can't resist a mystery. Boy, will she be surprised when she finds out what a big mystery this really is."

Just then, Vera and Julie came back into the kitchen. "The van is filled to bursting," Vera said, plopping down at the kitchen table. Her gaze lingered on the photo of Zach Caulder in his office.

"There are only a few more items," Julie added. "I can take those in my car."

"Oh, my!" Vera exclaimed suddenly, looking at the picture. "That box. I don't know why I didn't notice before. . . ."

"What is it?" Bess asked.

"It's the same box Rosemary Norris donated to be auctioned off today."

Nancy's mouth fell open. "You mean it's sitting out at the White Falls Inn, with all the other things for the auction?" she asked.

"I'm afraid so," Vera said. "Just about everything for the auction is already there. But let me make sure."

She got up and disappeared into the workroom. When she returned, she was carrying a small pamphlet. "Here's the catalog for the auction," she said. "I've been making notations on it to keep track of what's where." Vera quickly consulted the catalog. "Here it is. Yep. Mrs. Norris had that box of poems delivered yesterday afternoon."

Nancy jumped up from the table. "You and I had better get over there right away, Vera," she said. "You guys can pack up the last things and meet us there, okay?"

Before anyone could answer, Nancy was pulling Vera out the door.

The rear door of the van was still open, and Nancy could see the black lacquered trunk and wooden captain's chest. "I never did thank you for getting those two trunks back for me," Vera said as she pulled the door shut. "I don't know what I would have done without you girls."

"Don't thank us yet," Nancy said. "We still haven't figured out who's after the money. And to make things worse, we might have lost Zach Caulder's diary."

Vera waved a hand. "Don't worry about it," she said. "It looks as if we're going to get to the money chest first. I'm sure the diary will turn up." Then her eyes lit up. "Hey, I've got an idea. Julie's familiar with the inventory for the museum. When all this is over, I'll have her look for it."

Something about Vera's words struck Nancy. Julie had said she didn't believe the theory about Zach Caulder's money being hidden. But when she'd looked at the picture of Zach in his office, she'd quoted his diary word for word, as if she were totally convinced there really was a secret money chest.

As Nancy and Vera set off in the van, Nancy's mind kept flashing on different images. The way Julie had been so strongly opposed to Bess's reading the diary, and how she hadn't wanted Bess to go up into Zach's office . . . It was almost as if Julie were hiding something. And then she'd been so set on convincing Vera that Roz was trying to sabotage her, even after it became clear that the thief was after Zach's money.

No one event had seemed that suspicious, but

together, it all added up. The only thing that didn't make sense was Julie being knocked out. Even this morning, the way Julie had quoted Zach's diary, it was as if she had just read it very recently. But that could only be possible if . . .

The truth hit Nancy with a sickening wave. "Oh, no," she said in a horrified whisper. "Vera, stop the van! We have to go back to your house right away!"

15

A Deadly Race

Shooting Nancy a puzzled glance, Vera said, "Are you sure it can't wait, Nancy? I thought we were in a hurry to get to the White Falls Inn."

"Julie's the one who's after Zach Caulder's money," Nancy said urgently.

"Nancy, stop talking nonsense—" Vera's voice broke off suddenly, and Nancy saw a look of fear come into her eyes. Vera was pumping the brake furiously, but the van kept moving. It rounded the first curve in the road at an alarming speed.

"Nancy, the brakes don't work!" Vera cried. Her knuckles were white from holding the steering wheel so tightly.

Vera's face lost all its color as the van picked up

speed, careening down the road. They whipped around a curve, and the van tilted dangerously to the side, its wheels screeching loudly. Nancy had to grip her seat to keep from falling into Vera's lap.

Nancy's mind raced. There was no possible course for them except to continue down the sharply curving road. She had to find a way to stop the van before they tipped over or crashed into something.

Her eyes flew up ahead. "There's a snowbank up by the next curve," she said to Vera, trying to keep her voice calm. She pointed to a high wall of snow that looked as if it had been left by a snowplow. "Steer into it."

Without taking her eyes off the road, Vera nodded. A moment later, Nancy braced herself against the dashboard as the van slid into the snow. It came to a jerking stop.

"Phew!" Vera smiled weakly and turned to Nancy. "I don't know what could have gone wrong. I've never had a problem with the brakes before."

Nancy frowned. "I don't like the looks of this, Vera. I want to check something."

Nancy got out of the van. Scooping away some of the snow, she bent to look underneath the van. Immediately she saw what the problem was. The brake line leading to the front right tire had been cleanly cut.

She brushed the snow from her jeans and got back into the van. "Julie cut the brake cable," she said grimly.

Vera's expression darkened. "You're wrong, Nancy," she said. "Julie would never do this to me."

Taking a deep breath, Nancy said, "Think about it, Vera. Julie was the first one to go outside this morning. She left the kitchen very suddenly"— Nancy gave Vera a meaningful glance—"right after we figured out that the carved box from Esther Grey's house could be Zach Caulder's money chest."

"But why?" Vera asked. She still didn't look convinced, but Nancy detected a note of uncertainty in her voice.

"She's after Zach Caulder's money, and she wanted to make sure we couldn't do anything to stop her," Nancy replied. She quickly explained all the ways Julie had tried to mislead them earlier.

Vera shook her head. "But, Nancy, Julie was knocked unconscious. How do you explain that?"

"I can't—yet," Nancy said, frowning. "But everything else fits. Charlie and Mike couldn't have moved those trunks over to Roz's office without a car. But Julie has a car. All she had to do was use the dolly to get the trunk out of the workroom. She was in your house alone right before both trunks were taken. And she's the only other person besides us who comes and goes from the house a lot. She could easily have taken the diary from Bess."

Nancy sighed in frustration. "The worst thing is, I just told her exactly where to find Zach Caulder's money."

Then Nancy gasped as an even worse thought occurred to her. "Bess and George are alone with Julie!" She threw open the van's door and jumped out again. "We've got to make sure they're okay."

"Nancy, wait," Vera said urgently. "Julie's probably already on her way to the White Falls Inn. If we don't get there fast, she'll take the chest and escape before we can get there."

"We'd better split up," Nancy said. "Julie could be dangerous, so I'd better be the one to go after her. Still, I can't just leave Bess and George . . ."

"Don't worry, I'll be back at my house in less than a minute," Vera said, starting up the hill. Nancy opened her mouth to object, but Vera held up her hand. "I'll check the windows first. If Bess and George are in any kind of trouble with Julie, I'll call the police from the neighbors'."

Nancy smiled gratefully. "Okay," she said. "Tell the police to send a car to the White Falls Inn, too. And be careful!"

As Vera ran up the hill, Nancy raced down the curving road to Main Street. She waved to the first person who drove by, a farmer in a pickup truck.

Within minutes, he had dropped Nancy off at the White Falls Inn.

Nancy quickly scanned the parking lot, but she didn't see Julie's yellow car. Good, she thought—that meant she had beat Julie there.

A big red banner over the entrance announced the auction, which would take place in the inn's grand ballroom at two o'clock. Hurrying inside, Nancy asked a portly woman at the front desk to direct her to the ballroom.

"Just follow the signs," the woman said. She indicated a red arrow leading to a hallway off the lobby. "I'm afraid it's closed to the public until twelve-thirty, though. The auction is still being set up—"

Nancy didn't give the woman time to finish. She raced down the hallway to a set of huge double doors. A sign posted nearby confirmed that the ballroom was closed to the public until twelve-thirty.

Nancy tensed. Then, taking a deep breath, she pushed open the door and stepped inside.

To her surprise, the ballroom was empty. Rows of folding chairs had been set up in the front of the room. She hurried past them to the tables where the items were displayed, on the far side of the enormous ballroom. Her shoes echoed eerily on the ballroom's wooden floor.

"Where's that box?" she muttered. She searched

frantically among the furniture, wooden toys, quilts, ironwork, and other things to be auctioned off.

Just when she was beginning to think the box wasn't there, Nancy caught sight of the familiar ornately carved wood.

"Aha!" She swooped forward and picked up the heavy box. It was definitely the same one she had seen in Esther Grey's study the day before.

Her heart pounding in her chest, Nancy leaned against an open doorway at the rear of the ballroom.

She had just lifted the box's lid when she felt a prickling on the back of her neck. A fraction of a second later, a floorboard creaked in the doorway just behind her.

Before Nancy could turn around, a chilling voice said, "Thank you, Nancy."

Nancy whirled around and found herself face-to-face with Julie.

"You've just saved me the trouble of searching through all these dusty old things," Julie went on. "If you don't mind, I'll take that box now."

The young blond woman was staring at Nancy with an almost demonic smile. Nancy gulped when she saw what Julie was holding in her hand. It was a large butcher knife, and its sharp, pointy end was aimed right at Nancy!

16

Terror at the Factory

Nancy took a step back from Julie. Keeping her eyes on the knife, she said carefully, "Vera's already called the police, Julie. They'll be here any minute. Put the knife down."

Julie's short blond hair brushed her face as she shook her head. "I guess that means I'll just have to leave before I find out exactly how rich I am."

Shooting a warning look at Nancy, Julie added, "You'll be joining me, of course. You don't think I'd be dumb enough to leave you here, do you?" She gestured toward the ballroom's rear doorway with her knife. "Fortunately, this old inn has plenty of unused hallways, so no one will see us on our way out. Come on. We're getting out of here."

Not yet! Nancy wanted to scream. The police

would be arriving soon. She had to find a way to delay Julie a little longer. If she could only keep Julie talking . . .

"Where are Bess and George?" Nancy demanded. "What have you done with them?"

Julie gave a harsh little laugh. "There's no need to worry about your friends," she said. "They're safely locked in Vera's workroom."

Nancy hoped Julie was telling the truth.

"That was very clever, the way you tried to set up Roz Chaplin," Nancy went on, stalling for more time. Where were the police?

The corners of Julie's mouth barely lifted in an icy smile. "It was, wasn't it?" She waved the knife at Nancy again and said in a deadly tone, "Let's go—*now*."

With a sinking feeling in the pit of her stomach, Nancy stepped ahead of Julie into the hall. She couldn't help being acutely aware of the razor-sharp knife she knew was pointed at her back.

As Julie had predicted, there was no one else in the hall. Following the blond woman's instructions, Nancy walked to the end of the hall and out a back door.

Stay calm, Nan, she told herself. She strained her ears for the sound of sirens, but heard nothing.

Julie directed Nancy through a small stand of trees to her yellow car, which was parked on the street behind the inn. Opening up the hatchback,

Julie took out a length of rope and quickly tied Nancy's wrists together behind her back. Then she opened the passenger door and pushed Nancy roughly inside.

"Where are we going?" Nancy asked.

"My original plan was to grab Zach's money and be far from White Falls before anyone even knew it was gone," Julie said, ignoring Nancy's question. "You've botched up that plan. Now I'm going to make sure you don't ever cause me trouble again."

She placed the carved chest in the backseat and slid in behind the wheel, resting the butcher knife in her lap.

"Whatever you're planning, you won't get away with it, Julie," Nancy said as the car took off down the winding street.

"Why not?" Julie asked smugly. "You thought you were so smart. But you led me right to Zach Caulder's money and you didn't even know it."

Julie was heading down the hills, toward the river. Glancing behind her, Nancy noticed a woven bag on the seat next to the carved box. A familiar worn leather cover peeked out from the bag's edge.

"So you *did* take the diary back from Bess," she murmured.

Julie nodded. "I thought maybe there was some clue in it that I missed. There was no way I was going to let you three beat me to that money."

"You read about the money in Zach Caulder's diary before we got here, didn't you?" Nancy said. "That's why you were so upset when Bess wanted to read it. You didn't want anyone to find out about the money until you found it."

A wistful look came into Julie's eyes. "I'd just found out about the money the day you arrived," she said. "Too bad the money wasn't in one of those other trunks. I would have been far away from White Falls before you ever figured out what was going on."

"But why did you bother moving the trunks?" Nancy asked. "Couldn't you have just examined them at Vera's?"

Julie frowned. "Vera's the one who usually goes through the donated things. All I do is input the lists she makes into the computer. I was afraid she might have gotten suspicious if she saw me inspecting the things."

"So you took the trunks," Nancy went on. "And when you didn't find Zach Caulder's money, you decided to make it look like Roz had stolen them. Meanwhile, you kept looking for the real money chest."

Julie let out an amused laugh. "Actually, Vera gave me the idea herself when she was telling you about Roz's opposition to the museum. Everyone knows how much Roz detests Vera. Once I heard that you were going to be keeping an eye on Roz, I decided to make sure she appeared as guilty as Vera already thought she was."

"Vera trusted you," Nancy said angrily. "How could you turn against her like this?"

Nancy thought she detected an uneasy glint in Julie's green eyes. "I wasn't trying to hurt her," the blond woman said after a short silence. "But I deserve this money. I'm the one who found out that it was still around, not Vera. I should be the one to keep it."

"That money was Zach Caulder's, not yours," Nancy argued. "You don't have any right to it."

Julie's face reddened. "Keep quiet!" she cried, hitting the steering wheel with her palm. "You've already almost ruined everything. I'm not going to let you get in my way now."

Nancy fell silent, looking ahead through the windshield as Julie drove over the Deerfield River bridge. Nancy now had a good idea where they were going. Her suspicion was confirmed when the yellow hatchback pulled to a stop in front of Caulder Cutlery a few minutes later.

"There's still one thing I don't understand," Nancy said as Julie reached into the backseat and grabbed the carved chest.

The chest in one hand and the knife in the other, Julie got out of the car and went around to the other side. "What's that?" she asked as she opened the passenger door and gestured with the knife for Nancy to get out. Her anger seemed to have faded to a chilly calmness again.

"When we found you in Vera's workroom the day we arrived, you were really unconscious," Nancy said, looking curiously at Julie.

Julie stared at Nancy for a long moment. "I guess it can't hurt to tell you," she said finally. "I didn't plan on getting knocked out. It was an accident. I was so excited when I read about the money chest in Zach's diary that I tore the workroom apart looking for the chests."

She smiled to herself. "That's when I took the black lacquered trunk home—I was pretty sure it had been donated along with the diary. It was only later that I checked the records and realized that the other chest—that wooden one—had also been Zach's."

"That still doesn't explain how you got knocked out," Nancy pointed out.

"Well, by the time I got back to the workroom after taking that first trunk, I knew Vera would be back any second," Julie explained. "I had to really rush to get everything back in place. I guess I must have knocked something from one of the shelves by accident, and it hit me on the head."

Nancy nodded, remembering the cast-iron weather vane she'd found on the floor near Julie.

"And when I woke up, you were all leaning over

me," Julie went on. "I was sure you knew what I'd done. Then I realized you thought someone *else* had knocked me out, so I just went along with it."

The blond woman laughed mockingly at Nancy. "Boy, did I have you fooled!" In the next instant, Julie's face became an icy mask as she added, "And I'm about to fool everyone again."

She shoved Nancy toward the entrance to the factory. Then, using her key, she opened the double doors and gestured for Nancy to go inside.

"Down to the cellar," Julie instructed. She smiled at Nancy. "It's time to pay another visit to Charlie Shayne. He doesn't know it yet, but he's about to commit another murder."

Nancy shot a quick look over her shoulder. "What do you mean?" she asked.

Waving the knife with a little flourish, Julie said, "Why, your murder, of course. It's a shame that such a talented detective has to die at the hand of a deranged killer. Everyone will think that Charlie Shayne couldn't resist returning to the scene of the crime to kill again."

"You know Charlie wouldn't hurt anyone," Nancy protested. "Why don't you leave him out of this? If anything happens to me, my friends will know that you did it, not Charlie."

Julie's only answer was to shove Nancy across the main floor toward the staircase. With her hands tied, Nancy barely managed to keep her balance on

144

the narrow stairs. She made as much noise as she could, trying to alert Charlie. Maybe he could blockade himself into the little room.

But Julie didn't lose a moment. As soon as they reached the basement, she hurried to the far wall, pushing and pulling the shelves until she found the one that concealed the doorway to the smaller second room.

"Charlie, look out. She has a knife!" Nancy shouted as Julie pushed her into the other room.

In a glance, Nancy saw that Charlie's makeshift bed was empty, as was the rickety wooden chair where he'd been sitting when Nancy saw him the night before. The old man wasn't there.

Relief flooded through her. At least now Julie couldn't get Charlie mixed up in her devious plan. Turning to Julie, she said, "It looks like your plan won't work after all."

Julie frowned as she surveyed the room. "This is just a minor inconvenience," she said. "Whether Charlie's here or not, the evidence will point his way if the knife and your body are discovered with his things."

Nancy shivered at the word *body*.

In the next instant, Julie put the chest down and turned to face Nancy, holding up the butcher's knife. "Say goodbye, Nancy Drew."

17

A Secret Unveiled

Nancy's gaze flew from the knife to the carved box on the floor.

"Julie, are you sure it's worth killing me?" Nancy asked in the calmest voice she could manage. "You haven't even checked to make sure the money's really in that chest."

Julie hesitated, looking uncertainly at the box.

"Get over in that corner," she ordered Nancy, waving toward the farthest place from the doorway. "I don't want you trying anything sneaky while I'm opening this."

Once Nancy had obeyed, Julie kneeled on the floor next to the box, facing her. First Julie dumped all the papers from the carved chest. Nancy saw that, although the box was about a foot deep on the outside, its inside cavity was only half that.

Julie pushed at the end panels of the box, until one of them finally moved to the side. Nancy couldn't see clearly, but the angry look on Julie's face told her something was wrong.

"A lock!" Julie muttered angrily. "That Caulder guy really didn't trust anyone, did he?"

"Imagine that," Nancy said sarcastically. Taking a step to the side, she was able to see the small, rusty lock hanging from a hinge just behind the false panel.

Julie looked furtively around the room. "Aha!" she said, darting over to the windowsill. She picked up the cast-iron candle holder. "This will do." She went to work on the lock with such energy that Nancy thought she might hurt herself.

Suddenly, out of the corner of her eye, Nancy caught a slight movement in the doorway. She did a double take as she saw Charlie Shayne's grizzled, gray-haired head. Nancy opened her eyes wide and shook her head in the tiniest nod, warning him not to enter.

From the cautious way Charlie was eyeing Julie, Nancy guessed that he had already sized up the situation. As his eyes met hers, Charlie winked and put a finger to his lips. Julie, intent on breaking the lock, didn't seem to have noticed a thing.

Nancy started to edge slowly around the room toward the doorway. Alone, with her hands tied behind her back, there hadn't been much hope of her getting away. But now that Charlie was here—

"*Yes!*" Julie crowed triumphantly, breaking into Nancy's thoughts.

Julie tossed the broken lock to the floor and feverishly threw open the latch, pulling at the inside panel. A piece of yellowed paper was wedged into the opening behind the panel. Julie quickly threw the paper aside.

As the blond woman let out a gurgle of pleasure, Nancy looked back at the box. She could hardly believe her eyes. The secret compartment was completely filled with money. Julie had pulled out a fat wad of hundred-dollar bills and was staring at them as if she were in a trance.

Nancy knew it was now or never. Sprinting the last few feet to the doorway, she quickly squeezed through. Then she used her weight to spin the shelf-door closed, locking Julie inside the room.

"Help me block the door!" she shouted to Charlie, but he was already next to her, his burly arms braced firmly against the shelving.

A moment later, they felt Julie banging against the door and heard her muffled shouting. "Let me out! I won't hurt you, I swear!"

Charlie looked at Nancy and grinned. "What do you say, Miss Nancy Drew? Do you believe her?"

"No way," Nancy replied emphatically. The sounds of approaching sirens told her that the police had finally found them. Within minutes officers were racing down to the cellar. Nancy recognized one of them as Margaret Conroy. They were followed quickly by Vera, Bess, and George.

"Nancy, you're all right!" Bess cried as the cousins hugged her.

"I've never been happier to see you guys in my life," Nancy said as George untied her wrists. "Julie didn't try to hurt you, did she?"

Bess shook her head. "We were only locked in the workroom for a few minutes before Vera found us."

"Speaking of locked in . . ." Nancy turned to Officer Conroy and nodded toward the shelf-door. "I believe the person you're looking for is right in there, Officer."

"Everything is set," Vera said two hours later as she and Mrs. Norris joined Nancy, George, and Bess at the back of the big old-fashioned ballroom of the White Falls Inn. "When Esther Grey's poems go on the block in a few minutes, I'm going to tell the whole story of the money box and the old murder."

The auction was already under way. The rows of folding chairs Nancy had seen earlier were now filled with people bidding on items at the front of the room. The auctioneer, a thin, spindly man, was rattling off the bids while two helpers held up a patchwork quilt.

Mrs. Norris shook her head sadly. "I never would have thought Esther could actually kill someone." Vera had taken Mrs. Norris aside and explained everything when she and the girls had arrived at the auction. "But the letter that was found with the money proves it. The public has a right to know what really happened."

After the police had taken away Julie, Nancy, Vera, Bess, and George had gone back into the factory's hidden room. That was when Nancy had picked up the yellowed paper Julie had tossed from the opening of the secret compartment. She and her friends had been completely surprised by what they read on the paper.

Nancy nodded to where Mike and Grace Shayne were sitting at the end of a row of chairs. "I'm glad the Shaynes are here to see Charlie vindicated," she said.

"Oh, yes," Vera agreed. "I've already told them. Grace was so relieved to hear that her relative is not a murderer. She actually smiled."

"I bet she and Mike were pretty happy to hear that you plan on making Charlie the caretaker of the museum when it opens," George said.

"It's the least I can do to thank him," said Vera. "He may have saved Nancy's life."

Bess pointed to the front of the ballroom, where

Roz Chaplin was sitting. The real estate developer wore a look of complete indifference as she watched the quilt being auctioned off. "Roz couldn't have been very happy to find out that her famous relative was Zach Caulder's killer, though."

Vera let out a low whistle. "That's for sure. I felt badly that I had to tell her such terrible news, especially after the way she helped me out today."

Nancy looked questioningly at Vera.

"Roz was the one who arranged to have the things in Vera's van brought over here," Bess explained. "Vera didn't know who else to call. As soon as Roz heard what the problem was, she sent over two guys and a big truck. She said she wanted people to know once and for all that she wasn't the person who was sabotaging Vera."

Nancy grinned at her old neighbor. "Maybe there's hope that you and Roz can become friends after all."

"Well, we won't be enemies, anyway," Vera said. "Oh—it's time," she added, getting to her feet.

Looking back at the platform, Nancy saw that the quilt had been sold. Zach Caulder's carved wooden chest rested on a pedestal, its lid open to reveal Esther Grey's poems. For now, the secret compartment was closed.

Vera walked up to the platform and took the microphone from the auctioneer. "As you all know, a collection of Esther Grey's love poems is next to be auctioned off. We had originally intended to sell the poems with the box Miss Grey always kept them in. Due to an amazing discovery, however, only the letters are for sale at this time."

Disappointed murmurs rose from the crowd. "What's going on?" a man in the middle of the room wanted to know.

"Just a few hours ago, key evidence to a fifty-year-old murder was discovered in this box," Vera told the audience. She went on to explain that Zach Caulder was the mystery man Esther Grey had been in love with, and that he had hidden his fortune in the carved wooden box. Then she announced that evidence had been found in the box to prove that Esther Grey was the one who killed Zach Caulder.

The ballroom erupted in exclamations of surprise. Vera held up her hand for silence.

"We can't show you the actual money," she said once everyone had quieted down. "It's in police custody for the moment."

Nancy leaned over to Bess and George. "Vera's petitioning to have the money used to turn Zach Caulder's factory into the historical museum," she whispered.

"Good," Bess whispered back. "Oh, look! Vera's opening the compartment."

Vera's dark eyes gleamed as she revealed the secret compartment and took the yellowed sheet of paper from it. "But I can read the letter that was

152

found with the money," she said. "It's dated just two weeks after Zach Caulder's death.

" 'To Whoever May Find This,' " Vera read. " 'I must unburden my soul of this terrible nightmare. Each night in my dreams, I relive the horror: my hand raised against Zachary, the evil glimmer of the knife, the look of terror in his eyes. And then it is done. I have put out the light of Zachary's life forever. I keep hoping this vision is but a dream, but I know my love is really gone.' "

There were shocked exclamations from the crowd. Then Vera continued reading:

" 'Why must Zachary mock me like this, even in death? Today I happened upon this secret compartment with its cache of money. How worthless his fortune is to me! It cannot bring my dearest Zachary back, nor erase the emptiness of my soul. I love him still, and remain in utter despair without him. Sweet Zachary, how could I have done this to you?' "

Vera looked up at the audience. "The letter is signed by Esther Grey," she finished. "It and the carved box will be on display in the White Falls Historical Museum when it opens next year."

The crowd sat in stunned silence as Vera left the platform and returned to the rear of the ballroom. Within moments, the room jumped to life as bids for Esther Grey's love poems were shouted out. Everyone wanted to buy the poems.

"Well, it looks as though your auction is a success, Vera," Nancy said as Vera joined them.

"I'm sure the money brought in today will give your museum a good start," Mrs. Norris added. "I bought a lovely old rocking chair for myself—I couldn't resist."

Vera was glowing. "Everything is perfect," she said. "The White Falls Historical Museum is back on track, Charlie Shayne is a new man, and Roz Chaplin and I are actually on speaking terms."

George nodded toward the podium, where the bidding for Esther Grey's poems was still going strong. "After today, I think you'll have to rewrite a few pages of White Falls history."

Vera looked warmly at Nancy. "We certainly will," she said. "Finally the truth can be told, and it's all thanks to Nancy Drew."